Always Bet on Black
The Brothers of Chi-Town, Book 4

CHERYL BARTON

Published by: Cheryl Barton Publishing, LLC

This book is a work of fiction and any references or similarities to actual events, real people, living or dead, or to real places, are intended to give the novel a sense of reality. Any similarities in names, characters, places and incidents are entirely coincidental.

For permission requests, write to the publisher, addressed to: "Attention: Permissions Coordinator," at the address below.

Cheryl Barton Publishing, LLC
P.O. Box 217
Abingdon, Maryland 210096-0217

Ordering Information:
Quantity sales.
Special discounts of this novel are available on quantity purchases by corporations, associations, and others. For details, contact the publisher at the address above. For orders by U.S. trade bookstores and wholesalers, please contact prez@crbarton.com

ISBN: 978-1-948950-21-3

Dear Reader,

What a delight it is to write this series! Each brother from Chicago has qualities that make them completely different from the other and yet you will find something in each of them that you will desire. Can you believe that we, together, you and I, are up to book 4? These fellas are serious about their women. Wouldn't it be a perfect world if all men cherished their women the way these guys do in this series? Let's take a look back at the first three books in the series.

First there was Carter Garrison in, *"I Can't Let Go"*. He'd only known unconditional love with Sienna and when he woke up and realized his life would never be the same without her in it despite his indiscretion, he fought with all that was in him to prove to her that their love was worth trusting him again.

Then there is Torrence Allen in, *"Swagger and Baggage"*, book 2 in the series. He assumed Reese Michaels was the same woman he'd dated back in college who didn't want to commit to one man and so he didn't think of the impact their newfound love would suffer from his baggage which showed up and showed out to claim him as hers. He wasn't ready for Reese's reaction, nor did he plan to give up on her. He was in it to win her heart back by any means necessary.

Then, there was the fire that couldn't be doused in book 3 of the series, *"Claiming His Child"*. Dexter Patterson spent a lifetime never feeling loved, when as a child, he bounced from one unloving foster care home to another. It wasn't until he was faced with becoming a father, unexpectedly, that he realized he needed to open up his heart, not just to being a father without knowing what that meant, but also to being a man who was sorry for breaking the heart of the woman he found himself in love with but not yet ready to deal with it. To him, falling in love with Alyssa Kincaid wasn't easy, but he wouldn't change it for anything – not even when they both suffered from doubt and trust issues. Despite that, he had to find a way to deal with his past in order to live in the here and now and do it with the kind of love he didn't know was in him.

You are officially ready for book 4, of the series, *"Always Bet on Black"* where Delvin "DJ" "Black" Michaels finds that he can't escape the woman who stole his heart and without realizing it, at the same time, she drew him into her world of crime and trickery causing him to lose his job as a New York City police officer. The loss wasn't because of anything he did, but for what he witnessed that could take down an entire police force. To escape the wrath of his choice of a bed-mate, "DJ" returns to Chicago where he thought he could start his life over again as head of security at a casino owned by his future brother-in-law. Before he gets his feet wet in his new position, he comes face to face with a woman he knew as Justice Cooper, whose real name is Avalon Hart. If he thought he found her irresistible in New York, he's doomed now that she's in Chicago, enticing him with a mere look from her hazel eyes while reminding him with her sexy body of the nights they ravaged each other, forgetting the outside world existed. He knows of her history, but he still can't let go of the steamy nights they shared and he realizes that she wasn't done with him yet – not with his body nor with his heart.

When you're done falling in love with DJ and Avalon's story, get a quick look into Councilman Tucker Glass as he tangles with two women in his life who are both vying for the position of First Lady; one wants to be First Lady of Chicago while the other wants to be the First Lady in his life. He can only choose one – I wonder who it will be?

Thanks, as usual for taking this ride with me. The marathon continues with three more books after book 5 and then it will be time to exhale and take it all in. I hope you are loving this ride along with me. Let's go! Happy Reading!

Introduction

From last chapter of "Claiming His Child", book 3 of "The Brothers of Chi-Town" series.

The party at the casino was in full swing. Everyone was in their best after five attire. Dexter was standing off to the side of the black jack table with Torrence and Carter while Alyssa and Reese played a few hands.

"Love, huh? You finally said it?" Carter asked.

"I did and I've been saying it every day," Dexter said.

"Oh, not only are you saying it, you're saying it loud and clear with that massive ring on her finger. You made me look bad with the size of that thing. I'll have to upgrade Sienna's ring just to keep up with you!" Carter joked.

"I would have given her any ring she wanted as long as she marries me in a few weeks," Dexter said.

After buying an engagement ring they both loved, Dexter was happy that they decided on a date that was coming up in just three short weeks. The ceremony was going to be a small, intimate affair and would coincide with her brothers being in town and her parents would also be returning to stand with them. Dexter was excited that his sister and her family would be joining them as well as Annie, the only mother he could relate to.

After taking Devon to meet her, Annie had been calling several times a week to hear the baby babbling through the phone. When he opened up his heart to love, he extended it to Annie, forgiving her for things that had happened many, many years ago, deciding to focus more on the future than the past.

"I'm happy for you, bro. Alyssa is perfect for you. She's got you grinning like a little boy all in love," Carter jested.

"Whatever. I'd grin like that again and again. Have you seen how beautiful my woman looks tonight? That's all love, man," Dexter exclaimed, winking at Alyssa when she looked his way.

"I know what you mean," Torrence said. "I can't wait to love Reese for the rest of my life. Looks like our anniversaries will be three months apart. We'll have to plan trips in the future as couples to celebrate our dates together," Torrence added.

"Is DJ walking her down the aisle? I know there is some tension with her father, not with her as much as it is with DJ and their father," Carter asked. "Speaking of her brother, I'm still trying to figure out if we're still calling him DJ or Black or Delvin? How is he working out as head of security? What name is he using professionally? Isn't this his first full week?" Carter asked.

"It is and so far, he's doing great. He prefers to use the name *"Black"* and that's what we're going by. For some reason, he still hates the name Delvin, his given name. It's about the bad blood and being named after a father he hates. He's whipping his team into shape. He's coming this way now," Torrence said, waving Black over.

"DJ! What's up, brother?" Carter asked, greeting him.

"Nothing much. Trying to make sure no one is stealing from Torrence," he joked.

"I bet your family is happy to have you back in Chicago. You didn't like New York?" Dexter asked.

"There was a lot about New York I did like, but it wasn't the place for me. I need familiar territory. Besides, I let a lady take me down, something I haven't told Reese about, so don't let on. It was bad stuff," DJ whispered as if he thought someone would hear them.

Dexter looked between Carter and Torrence and wondered if either of them knew the story.

"How bad is bad?" Carter asked.

"Not bad enough that I didn't give him the job as head of security. What happened wasn't his fault and he's in Chicago looking for a fresh new start," Torrence said.

He smiled over at DJ, letting him know that he had his back. He'd been on the other end of loving a woman who didn't really love him back, but unlike him, in the end, DJ didn't end up with his woman the way Torrence had.

"So, you know what happened, Torrence?" Dexter asked.

Torrence looked to DJ who gave him a nod that meant it was okay to share with this small group. He knew that DJ had been gone for several years and being back in Chicago, he didn't want to reconnect with his old crowd, a reason for leaving the city in the first place and what he knew DJ needed most was a group of positive brothers to be around to help keep him from slipping back into his old ways before he joined the New York Police Department.

"I do. I went to New York to help him out of a situation.

Reese wanted me to connect with him because she said she felt that he needed a friend he could trust and not those clowns in New York. There is so much corruption there and Black got caught up in it trying to do the right thing. Some guys on the force were trying to set him up in a sting and it involved this young woman. Black got wrapped up and it was a whole thing and I do mean a big thing. So big that it was kept out of the press – that's how big that situation was. I'll let Black share more if he wants," Torrence said.

They all looked to Black. Like Carter and Torrence, Dexter waited to see how much he would share.

"I'll tell you what, if you fellas would invite me for one of your pool games, I'll tell you about it. Thankfully, I got out of New York unscathed and all that was damaged was my pride and that took a major hit. You know it can be when you let a woman get the best of you and you end up lowering your guard," Black said.

"Yes!" Carter, Dexter and Torrence shouted together and then laughed out loud, collectively.

"Hey, what am I missing?"

They all turned around to Jermony walking up to them, also decked out in a black tuxedo for the night.

"Well, if it isn't Jermony Jeffries, one the country's top professional ball players. No game this weekend?" Carter asked.

"No. I wanted to be here for Torrence's event tonight and let me say, this place is jumping. From the concert with Mary J. Blige, which was on point as usual whenever she hits the stage and then there is this VIP party on the first-floor of the casino level which is off the charts!" Jermony exclaimed. "Where are your women at?" he asked.

"Sienna is at home relaxing. She isn't up to going out in her first months of pregnancy. If she hadn't forced me out of the house, I would have stayed in with her, but I think I was getting on her nerves asking her how she was feeling every few minutes. Seeing her go through pregnancy is beautiful and scary at the same time especially with morning sickness that seems to last all day," Carter explained.

"Right. I remember what she went through with Symone. Tell her I asked about her. She and Kimberly bonded over their stories of going through morning sickness," Jermony said. "What about Alyssa? Is she here with you?" he asked Dexter.

Dexter pointed to the table where she stood with Reese. Both must be winning when he noticed them pumping their fists in the air.

"She's at the tables playing black jack with Reese," he said.

"Who has Devon? You need to bring him and come to one of my home games. I like to secure the club level for my guests so the noise of the crowd doesn't scare my kids. Feel free to bring Devon anytime. I know he's still young, but because of my kids, we also have lots of entertainment for them, since the game is the last thing kids are interested in," Jermony said.

"I may do that. Thanks for the offer. Devon is with Sienna since Alyssa wanted to get out tonight or trust me, we would not be here tonight. She doesn't like to leave him too much and honestly, neither do I. We both needed a night out after focusing so much energy on combining our two houses into one," Dexter stated.

"Right. I heard about the move and that reminds me that

I wanted to talk to you," Jermony said to Dexter.

"Yeah? What's up?" Dexter asked.

"Carter said that you were thinking of subletting Alyssa's apartment since she and Devon moved in with you last week. I'm looking for a place for my sister to live. I offered to let her stay at my house, but she doesn't want to do that. I thought maybe she could sublet Alyssa's place until I have time to find her a more permanent spot if she decides to stay here in Chicago. I have to get back on the road in a few days for an away game and I don't have time to go with her to check out a lot of places right now. I understand where Alyssa was living has great security," Jermony said. "I want her here in Chicago, but I don't have the time to deal with that until the season is over. Kimberly would help, but she won't because she's still skeptical about my sister's appearance here in Chicago. She's going to need some time."

"Really? I got you, so don't worry about it. I hadn't put the word out about the sublet since we just finished moving the last of her stuff out a week ago. If you want it, it's yours. At least I know I'll get the rent," Dexter kidded. "There's a few months left on the lease," he said.

"I'll have my accountant write you out a check and deliver it to you tomorrow. Text me the rent and I'll pay out the rest of the lease to you. How's that?" Jermony asked.

"It's so good knowing people with money!" Dexter shouted and shook hands with Jermony sealing the deal.

"Hey, where is Kimberly tonight? Your wife is usually with you?" Carter asked. "You usually don't come to events like this without her," he said.

"True, not usually, but guess what? I have my sister with me tonight. She had been living in New York and had gotten herself into some kind of scandalous mess. I moved her here the other day and I thought she should get out and meet some higher caliber people than those she's been used to. I have a lot to catch you guys up on. Things have been pretty crazy since I connected with her," Jermony said.

Dexter looked around.

"Where is she?" he asked. "I've been looking forward to meeting her."

"She's around here somewhere," Jermony replied and looked around to see if he could spot her. He was surprised that for someone new to Chicago, she seemed to already know quite a few people.

"Seems like New York is a trouble spot for a lot of people. Jermony, you remember Reese's brother, DJ, but everyone calls him Black. You met him a few times years ago when he was still a youngster," Carter said, pointing Black out to him.

"Yeah, hey man," Jermony said greeting him. "It's good to see you again. You were a kid the last time I saw you."

"Yeah, I remember meeting you a few times years ago. I went to a few of your games with my sister. You play a mean game of basketball. I wish we had a team that supported you better," DJ said.

"Yeah, from your lips to God's ears!" Jermony joked.

"Team is better than it was last season, that's for sure," Dexter added.

"Hey Carter, you said something about trouble for a lot of people. What do you mean?" Jermony asked.

Carter looked to Torrence then to DJ and seeing no sign that he couldn't share the bare minimum, he turned to Jermony.

"DJ here was just telling us about some trouble he was in

as a New York City police officer. He's back here living in Chicago, too, and is now head of security here at the casino. New York is a hot spot, it seems," he said.

"You made it out okay?" Jermony asked DJ.

"Barely. There was this woman who used me to get some inside information and I was dumb enough to reveal what I should not have and it cost me my job. I got away from New York and from her as fast as I could," DJ explained.

"Did they catch the woman? Whatever it was, it was definitely kept on the low-low. Was she involved in something illegal?" Carter asked.

"Was she? It was crazy and because it involved some of the top cops in the city, it was all brushed under the rug, which is why the scandal didn't reach here to Chicago. Whoever this woman really is, she had people in high places who cleaned it all up for her," DJ explained.

"Wow, that's crazy," Carter said.

"It was. I was there with him for a short period of time before coming back here to Chicago and that mess was cleaned up with a quickness. Black coming back here to Chicago was the best decision he could have made. There was nothing was drama left for him if he'd stayed in New York and from what he has told me about this young woman he was involved with, she had heads swirling all over New York, including his," Torrence said.

"She must have been some woman if she hemmed you up like that," Dexter expressed.

"She was, but I'll never let a woman do that to me again and I do mean never!" DJ said.

"Sounds like a big mess and it's so coincidental. My sister was in some mess too that was out of this world crazy.

I'm still trying to get to the bottom of things, but she only gives me pieces here and there. In fact, here she comes now," Jermony said, waving her over as she walked in his direction.

Everyone turned around as a stunningly beautiful woman with long flowing natural hair and an hour-glass shaped glided up to them. Before anyone could be introduced, DJ shouted.

"You! What the hell are you doing here?" he asked pointedly and with anger so fierce, it was felt around their group.

Dexter was stunned along with Carter and Torrence. The young woman went from smiling at Jermony to glaring at DJ.

"Me! What are you doing here?" she asked loudly with her hair flying about as her head moved from side to side.

When DJ turned toward her to be more direct, Dexter started to move when he saw Jermony position himself between the two of them.

"Whoa – what the hell is this?" Jermony asked. "Why are you shouting at my sister?" he said to DJ as he put up his arms to keep distance between them all.

"Your sister? She's your sister?" DJ shouted and pointed at her.

"Yeah. This is Avalon Hart. We have the same father, but different mothers. How do you know him, Avie?" Jermony asked turning to her as his head looked around the entire group. He looked at Torrence who had also moved a little close, clearly in protective mode over DJ.

"Calm down DJ and let's all pull back our tempers before this gets out of control," Dexter said, trying to diffuse what appeared to be a situation on its way to being out of control.

"Avalon? Avie? Who is that? That's not her name. In New York, her name was Justice Cooper. Who is Avalon?" DJ asked, his voice getting louder as people around them turned to look in their direction.

"What?" Jermony asked as he turned to her. "Avie, what is he talking about? You know him and why does he know you as Justice Cooper? Who is that?" he inquired.

"Hey, let's cool it," Dexter said, always the negotiator who hates confrontation. He, like everyone else, turned to Jermony's sister as her shock turned to sassiness. The moment her hands went to her hips and she leaned her head to the side, he knew things were about to get interesting. He'd seen that look and it wasn't a good one.

"Well, it's fancy running into you *here*. I thought I left you back in New York," she said facetiously.

"Yeah, I bet you did. You thought you left me there to pick up after the mess you caused," DJ said in a way that made his words sound as if he were spitting them out.

"Avie? I asked you what's going on? I'm not an audience to this show, so explain!" Jermony said, his voice getting louder as well.

"We were in New York together and now we're in Chicago at the same time. This is going to be fun!" Avalon laughed. "This is too much for me and right now, I need a drink," she said and walked away.

As she did, DJ watched her every move. His eyes never left her as she walked a few feet away and then turned around and winked at him. No one else knew what it meant when she took her thumb, licked the pad of it and then pressed it to her behind. The moment she did so, his entire body jumped to attention. That one small act took him back to their time in New York when she had him wrapped around her finger. That one little movement she'd just made was done when she was naked except for a pair of high-heeled black strappy heels. With that thumb, she had branded herself, specifically her plump behind as his and dared him to come get what he wanted. He did over and over and over again.

Tonight, she was tempting him and his body remembered all of the delicious things they'd done together. He was drawn to her beauty once again until he snapped out of his trance and remembered that her behind had gotten him in the worse trouble of his life. He had to find a way to resist her magnetism. She was like a snake charmer and he was the snake making moves under her command.

"Black, what's going on?" Carter asked.

Remembering where he was, DJ snapped out of his trance and diverted his attention away from her and refocused.

"That's the woman who set me up! She's the reason I lost my job as a New York cop. She was part of a major ring that involved a large portion of the top leadership on the force, including the commissioner and she got me caught up. She's who they called the *Black Widow* because she took me down; she took down Black," he explained.

"That beautiful woman?" Dexter asked.

"My sister?" Jermony chimed in.

"Yeah, here. And now, to my dismay, she's here in Chicago. No disrespect Jermony, but your sister is a criminal and if she's here in Chicago, it's not just because you moved her here. Trust me, she's up to something and whatever it is, it's bad. I hope she isn't planning something here at the casino. I let her take me down once, but you know what, as the saying goes, always bet on *Black*. I'm on to her and I'll be watching."

"Look, I don't know what's going on here, but I'm going to go talk to my sister to get to the bottom of this and for now, stay away from her. I don't know what you think she did to you or anyone else, but it's not true and whatever happened is over. I got her out of it and she's doing all the right things now. I don't know all that she did and I don't care. I had my people on it and she's free and clear and I want to keep it that way. Stay clear of her," Jermony warned him.

DJ shrugged it off and turned and walked away before anyone could comment. He didn't have to be warned to stay away from her. She was his Kryptonite and if he was planning on keeping his sanity and his job, he knew to stay away. He only wished his body would forget about her as much as he was making his head do. He had put on a strong front for the guys, but inside, his heart was racing a million miles a minute. He tried to erase everything that Justice or Avalon, whatever she was calling herself, did to him. What he didn't tell them was that he was in love with her and he was in trouble. That love had taken him down before and if he didn't watch himself, it would happen again.

Heading toward the security office, DJ was almost to the elevator when Justice appeared in front of him with her perfectly polished finger nail resting between her teeth, looking at him with the look of innocence that originally drew him to her. That innocence had always gotten a rise out of him in more ways than one. Inhaling and exhaling to deal with her being close to him, he locked eyes with her.

"Why are you here, Justice?" he asked between clinched teeth.

"*Avalon*. My name is Avalon," she said in a soft, sexy tone that had him thinking of all the times she whispered his name while he made love to her in a car, in a bed, against a tree; so many places. The memories hit him like a flood. She was a drug to him and even now, he was barely resisting her.

"Okay, *Avalon*. What are you doing here?" he asked.

When she sidled up close to him, DJ didn't move away. He stood his ground even though that part of him that recognized her sexy voice stood at attention. When she looked down, he knew she saw it too because she smiled like she'd just won a prize. She knew what she was doing to him.

"Well, apparently I arrived just in *time*. Looks like one of my reasons for being here is clear. I bet you have a private room here at the casino we could slip off to. Remember how you like to do it standing up and sliding my thong to the side?" she asked. She leaned in closer. "Guess what I'm wearing under my dress?" she whispered.

DJ stood back to put some distance between them.

"I'm not falling for you and your tricks again. I was off my guard in New York, but not here in Chicago. I can see right through your sexy smile, pouty lips and thumb on your ass cheek; yeah, I saw that. Don't try and play me with that foolishness. It won't work again," DJ said. Even as the words left his mouth, he could feel his resolve slipping away. When Avalon looked around and saw no one looking, she ran her finger from his chest down to his zipper.

"Should I call you Black or DJ, now that you're here in Chicago. In New York, you loved when I shouted your name while you were..."

"Stop it! I'm working and I don't have time for you right now," he said.

"Working?" she asked.

"I'm head of security here at the casino," he explained.

"Then I'll see you all the time. I like that. We could have fun. I know you're mad at me right now, but I can calm and warm you up. I'm staying at the Ritz-Carlton Hotel. The room is under my brother's name and I'll be there all night tonight, all by myself. I can help you with that. No strings," Avalon said, gazing down at his zipper before walking away.

DJ couldn't think of any quick wit words to come back with. His eyes were too focused on he behind as she walked away.

"I'm in trouble and her name is Avalon Hart," he said as the elevator door opened and he quickly got in. Why was he so weak when it came to her? She had destroyed his life and all he can think about was how quickly he could divest her of her evening gown to get inside of her knowing the things she could do with her hips. Even now, he was wondering how he could slip away from the casino to visit her hotel room.

His recent history was already repeating itself, but even if he decided to indulge in her sweetness, he wouldn't lose focus on the fact that she had to be working on a new scheme and it's possible it included the casino. This time he would be ready for her. This time, he was betting on *Black* to come out on top.

Prologue
New York City
1 Year Ago

"Your hand is on my thigh."

The strain in DJ's voice wasn't the only strain he was experiencing. The fact that the light touch of Justice's fingers on his right thigh made the hair on his legs tingle even through the layer of the pants of the tuxedo he wore. There was another strain against the zipper of his tuxedo pants that annoyed him. He hated that the very hot and sexy, Justice Cooper, could get control of him with just the slightest touch of her hand, pretty much anywhere on his body, but right now, he knew her intention and her plan was a devious one. She knew how to play him. He grimaced with a touch of delight at the sound of her chuckle, a sign that she knew the impact of her bright red-tipped fingernails as she moved them further up his thigh to that area where he usually loved for her hands to be, but not while he was driving through the streets of New York.

"*Delvin Michaels*! You don't like my hand on your thigh?" Justice asked. "Mmm, last night, you didn't a problem with my hand being a whole lot of places on your body. In fact, I can remember how we barely got an ounce of sleep. You were ravenous for me and I loved every second of it. I like how hot and animalistic my touch gets you and with the number of times we both climaxed, trust me, I know that you loved it too," she said.

DJ turned his head slightly to the left to look at her and then turned his head back to the highway in front of them as they sped through traffic to get to the Manhattan Center for a major event being hosted by the Police Commissioner of the New York City Police Department, Silas Oakes. He was still having a hard time believing he had actually received an invitation and the look of jealousy on the faces of his fellow officers who were not invited was enough to give him an ego boost that nothing could deflate.

He had been on the force for several years and had somehow garnered close friendships with not only the commissioner, but the Mayor and his police chief, at least over the past six months or so. He was riding high at the sudden interest in him by leadership and he was loving every minute of it. The highlight of his career was not work related, but was due to the beautiful woman who sat in the passenger seat of his rented gray-on-gray Mercedes E-Class, which he had secured just for this event. While he thought of his career and the sexy woman next to him, he just realized what she'd called him. That name made his skin crawl – even though it technically was his name. It still gave him nightmares. He was still considering changing his name to something that didn't give him reminders of who fathered him.

"You know I hate that name. I've told you the story behind why I don't like it. It reminds me too much of my father and I hate thinking about that coward," he scolded lightly and then smiled. It was her fault that his father wasn't someone he admired or even liked, but the fact that he had his name bothered him every time someone used it or even when he had to write it.

DJ clinched his teeth as Justice's hand moved even higher up his thigh and the look in her eyes told him all he needed to know. He was suddenly joining her in her thoughts and would like nothing more than to indulge, but he couldn't. He had to stay focused and they had someplace to be.

"But I love saying Delvin. I love how it rolls off of my tongue, across my lips and out of my mouth, like your name was meant to be whispered by me. You can't tell me you don't enjoy my lips," Justice said with so much sexual undertone that DJ didn't just hear her, but he saw the words roll across her tongue and across her lips – both parts of her that did delicious and sexy things to his body.

Even now, his body was reacting to the thought of the trouble he knew she was trying to get them into, even while in the car. His entire body stiffened and not just the member behind his zipper, which was well aware of her presence. Usually, it only took the mere thought of her or the scent of her sweet perfume or the feel of her soft, skin to have his body readying for any and everything she had in mind, and tonight was no exception, adding in the fact that he'd never seen a woman more wanton, sexy and desirable in a bright red evening gown with diamond accents that accentuated every single, magnificent curve he had come to love getting to know.

"I love it best when you call me *DJ* and you know that I'll damn near give you anything you ask me for when you call me, *Black*. I've never heard any woman say it with so much zeal and salaciousness like you do," he insinuated.

With another quick glance her way, he was about to leap out of his seat when he realized she'd moved one side of the strap of her gown down her shoulder, exposing one large, round breast. Her nipples stood at attention and his mouth watered remembering how she would writhed under him like a wild woman as he feasted on her, the way he was imaging doing right now. He was about to explode and was barely holding onto the little bit of control he still tried to maintain. When the car swerved to the left and the car in the next lane honked at him, he knew he had to get his mind right. He shook off any thoughts of finding a place to pull off to in order to get a little taste before the event. He'd never been tempted at this level by any woman before. There were days he barely made it through work after reading one sexy text after another from her while he was on patrol and he would damn-near go crazy when her text would be accompanied by a sexy picture. He needed to focus.

"Don't kill us in this car before you get a little taste of this before we get to the event," Justice said and laughed.

When Justice's fingers finally made their way to his erection, hard as steel behind his zipper, DJ knew they were in trouble because any minute he was about to not only lose control of the car, but of his body's reaction to her, not a first for him, just a first in a moving car. Then he thought about that and realized it wouldn't be the first time. There were a few times when he'd been driving them and she'd unzip him and lower her head to his lap. As a cop, if he knew that type of activity was occurring in a car, he would give the driver a ticket for indecency. Justice had him doing all kinds of things he shouldn't do, but he couldn't resist her. He'd never met a woman who was so free with her sexuality while also being secure in who she was. He tried to playfully swipe her hand away, which caused her to laugh even louder. From his side-eye, he could see her reaching up with her free hand to cup herself and he knew he could only take so much. He wanted her to stop while at the same time, he wished he could pull over and watch her the way he loved doing when they were alone in a place other than a moving car.

"You're trying to kill us, not me. My hand is on the steering wheel while yours is trying to get in all kinds of trouble and you know you need to stop enticing me and pull your dress back up. I don't need to say how hard it is for me to resist you, so stop it. We can't get into anything right now. I've never been invited to a gala this big where all the top levels of New York City and State government will be in the same place. I'm trying to make a good impression and being late with wrinkled clothes, smelling like I've just had wild sex is not the way to do it. Let me get us there in one piece and I promise, I will take care of you the second we get back to my place," he said, reaching down to remove her hand that had again found its way back to his leg.

DJ smiled when he watched Justice fix her dress, allowing him to exhale. She was just as sexy with her clothes on as she was completely naked, if not more-so. He was so close to going along with her plan. The sexy dress along with the even more sexier thong he knew she had on under it were enough to make him want to beg her to strip for him right in the car. He knew if she hadn't covered up, he would have to pull off the side of the road and give them both what they wanted and needed. They were non-stop ravenous for each other. He would definitely make time for that later, after the gala.

"You know, Delvin can be a prude. I want and need Black right now. Black would pull this damn car over and slide into me, not caring that we had someplace to be. I've got like three condoms in my bag and we could clean up right quick after. Black would do it, but I get that Delvin needs to get to the gala, so I'll let you have this one, but yeah, you are going to owe me. I'm picturing you paying up with my legs splayed out over both of your shoulders and all I want to see is your head moving around and around and up and down. You can be a prude, but I get it; only this one time. You know I love adventurous sex and just seeing you all dressed up in that black tuxedo is doing all kinds of nasty things to my mind and my body. We could pull off somewhere, take care of business and still get to the event on time, but I get it. You know you want to. When have you ever been able to resist me and the chance to have a quickie?" she asked.

DJ didn't answer because he hated that he couldn't resist her. He'd become someone he didn't recognize. All Justice had to do was bat those big, thick eyelashes at him or stick out her sexy, pouty lips and if she turned her body around, giving him a front seat view of her perfectly round behind, he was a lost cause. He had been that way since the moment they met over six months ago when she came on to him out of nowhere while he was on patrol.

Justice and some friends had been stranded with a broken down car and against police policy, he'd given them a ride to safety in his patrol car. He couldn't leave them in an area that he knew was a high-crime area. He could have waited with them for a tow truck, but the wait was over an hour and it was late in the evening. As Justice exited his car when he dropped them off, she had slipped him her number, which she had written on a piece of paper. She not only slip him her number, but she slid it down and into his pants pocket in a slow manner, making sure to let her hand rub slightly across the bulge he knew had already begun to form as he looked into her eyes and saw desire. When her soft hand came up and touched his, he knew he was done for. He tried to avoid calling her for an entire day and then gave up when her beautiful face plagued him as he slept and while he was awake.

Justice was the most beautiful woman he'd ever seen in his life and she was interested in him. That night, she wasn't provocatively dressed, but she glowed and she had a confident, take charge type of attitude that roped him right in. He wasn't anything to throw a stick at as far as his looks, as if he didn't deserve the attention of someone as beautiful as her and because of his good looks, something he wasn't vain about, but knew was fact, women approached him all the time. He had his share of women and was never without one if he wanted one in his bed or just on his arm. He'd recently broken off an engagement to a beautiful woman, but the situation wasn't right. Fresh out of that, he was up for some fun and in no time, Justice had become more than the fun he was seeking. She'd become so much more. He was in love with her, an unexpected surprise. He wasn't ready to be in love again, still getting over his last relationship and trying to regroup after that. Stopping at a light, he turned to her before it changed to green.

"Baby, I'm not trying to resist you, something you already know. We both know that's a losing game for me, so I don't waste time trying. I love everything about being with you, but we have the rest of the night and tomorrow after the gala tonight. I can take care all your needs, but first this and then that. I'm glad you talked me into going tonight. I was hesitant because of the bad blood this could cause between me and the other officers who were not invited, but I haven't had the best of luck befriending many of them. There is so much corruption and foolishness on the force that I try to get my shifts done and put that in my rear-view mirror until my next shift," he explained.

"I know. I try to help keep your mind off of work. What about Diego? You're close with him," Justice said.

DJ appreciated his friendship with Diego Santana. They were on the force together and if anyone had his back, it was him. They had become more than just co-workers.

"I am and I have a few other guys I'm cool with. Diego and I go out on a lot of calls together and he's like that big brother I've never had. This job is a lot some days and he's someone I can vent to because he understands the struggles of being a cop in New York," he explained. "He has his issues on the force too, so I try not to lay too much on him," he added.

"Well, I'm thankful for Diego. You told me if it wasn't for him telling you to call me, that we may not be together now. I'm still trying to fathom someone having to convince you to call *all of this*!" Justice joked.

DJ laughed when he looked at her as she used her hands to show that 'all of this' meant all of *her*. She was so beautiful, he couldn't believe he was lucky to have such an amazing woman as into him as he was into her. He was about to comment when he stopped as she checked her cell phone, which he knew had been vibrating like crazy since he picked her up at the apartment she shared with two other women – an apartment he was still trying to figure out how they could afford, when he still had no idea what any of them did for a living. Even on his salary, if he was getting paid twice the amount, he couldn't afford to live in the mid-city high-rise they shared.

"Important?" he asked, curiously.

"No. Just one of my roommates with a problem," she said.

"Do you need to call her back?" he asked, hoping she would share more. Justice had become very mysterious lately and he didn't know why.

He didn't want to mention that for the past week, he'd noticed that her cell phone would beep or vibrate and she never took calls when she was with him. He would see her step away to take a call or hang up suddenly if he walked up while she was on the phone.

"No, no, it's nothing. I'm going to turn it off," she said.

"What if it's really serious?" he asked, trying to get more information as his curiosity ran wild with what she was up to.

Justice didn't have a chance to answer as they pulled up near the Center and saw flashing red and blue lights all over the place. DJ looked around and knew that it wasn't because of the event, but something else was going on. As he pulled closer, he saw more than just New York City police cars and men, he saw men in FBI jackets.

FBI?

"Let's get out of here!" Justice screamed.

DJ turned to her and before he could reply, he was taken

back by the look of sheer terror on her face. She wasn't just scared that something horrible had happened like an accident, but something else was on her face. He could practically see her shivering in her seat as she looked wildly in all directions as if she was waiting for someone to show up at the car any second. He didn't want her to be afraid when he was around.

"I'm going to go see what's going on. I can't leave; I'm a cop," he shouted, pulling the car to the side of the road and taking out his badge so that it hung around his neck so that he could easily get closer when he encountered other police. He checked for his gun, which was on his hip but hidden by his suit jacket. Still, he felt better knowing where it was just in case there was a serious reason of why, what looked like the full force was in front of him.

When the car came to a stop, DJ reached for the door handle and halted when Justice gripped his forearm hard. He looked first down at where her hand gripped the jacket of his suit and then up to her face where her eyes had widened as they moved between looking at him and looking at the agents coming toward their car. He saw them too and knew that they would be safe when they saw his badge.

"No, DJ. Let's get out of here now! Please, *let's go*. Please, *please* just drive away!" Justice shouted in fear, trying to pull him so that he couldn't get out

He took note that she called him DJ; not Black and not Delvin, as she loved doing. She'd said DJ. She was afraid.

"What's wrong with you? You look like someone is about to murder you. I'll check this out and you can stay here in the car where you'll be safe with the doors locked – I *promise*," he encouraged as he again tried to get out of the car, only to still be held in her tight grasp.

"That...that's not it," Justice stuttered out. "Let's just go, *now*!" she screamed even louder.

Before DJ could answer to find out what she was so afraid of, he heard a loud knock on his car window and saw FBI agents standing on both sides of the car doors. He quickly rolled down the window on his side and produced his badge. He was about to announce who he was when the agent cut him off.

"I see your badge. Your name?" the agent asked.

"DJ, sorry, Delvin Michaels. I'm an officer on the New York City police force. What's going on?" he asked.

"And your lady friend, sir?" the agent asked.

"No," Justice said behind him softly. DJ turned in her direction and his words were halted when he saw tears flowing down her face. This wasn't just fear of what was happening at the end of the block; this was something else. Justice was displaying pure terror as she avoided looking at either agent.

"Sir? Officer Michaels? Her name, sir?" the agent asked again.

"Her name is Justice Cooper," he answered.

"Good – just checking for confirmation. Officer Michaels, I need you to step out of the car and away from Ms. Cooper, please. Ms. Cooper, please put your hands on the dashboard in front of you and don't move!" the agent shouted.

"What is going on? We're here for the event at the Manhattan Center. Why are you targeting her?" DJ asked, completely confused about what was going on.

"For starters, there is a situation that has unfolded

tonight and I'm afraid I need to take you and Ms. Cooper in for questioning," the agent on his side announced.

"What!" DJ shouted. "We just arrived. What are we being questioned about?" he asked.

"Agent Miller! She's here in this car and so is Officer Michaels. Send a woman officer over," the agent hollered at another agent who had been walking toward them and who quickly turned back around.

"I'm sorry, DJ," Justice said, so that only he could hear her. She wasn't looking at him. He found her looking down at her hands in her lap as she twisted them nervously.

He didn't know what to say or do and just watched as she lifted her hands and placed them on the dashboard as she was told.

"Officer Michaels, please step out of the car. I will explain everything. For now, we need you to answer some questions, but Ms. Cooper here, is under arrest."

DJ spun his head around so fast, he felt a slight crack as a tinge of pain shot down his spine.

"Under arrest? She's under arrest for what?" he asked.

He watched as the agent on the other side of the car opened the door on Justice's side. He was about to reach for her when the agent halted him.

"Don't, sir. Ms. Cooper, I'm sure is well aware of why we're asking her to step out and why she'll be placed in handcuffs. Please don't escalate the situation. I'm not sure of how much you know or don't know, but for now, please, just comply and we'll get this all settled."

DJ sat stoic and looked out over the steering wheel. He was dumbfounded. What is it that Justice supposedly knows?

"Ms. Cooper, please step out of the car and place your hands behind your back. I'll have a female officer here in just a second to escort you to a waiting car and you'll be taken to the downtown FBI office for questioning."

"Wait, wait!" DJ exclaimed, shaking his head to try and get his thoughts clear. He couldn't understand why Justice was being arrested. "What is going on?" he asked again.

"I'm sorry," Justice said again and exited the car.

DJ hopped out on his side of the car and attempted to walk around to her, but was stopped by the agent.

"Sir, you can't do that right now. Please don't say anything to her directly. You can address your questions to me. I may not be able to give you many answers right now, but I have to ask that you not say another word to Ms. Cooper."

DJ shook his head back and forth, trying to clear his thoughts and find some control over what he was seeing.

"Okay, tell me what's going on? What is she being charged with and why? Am I under arrest?" DJ asked.

"You'll both be taken in so that this can all be figured out. This is much bigger than you or Ms. Cooper, but from the look on her face, I take it, she knows that we were coming. Maybe not tonight, but she knew. Whether anyone will be charged remains to be seen. I will offer you both your rights, something you know all about, just so that I'm following protocol."

DJ stood still while their rights were read to them and his eyes stayed locked on Justice. She still wouldn't look at him. He turned when a female agent approached them.

"Ms. Cooper, do you have any weapons on your person, in this car or in your purse?" the officer asked her.

"No," she responded.

"Weapons? Why would she have a weapon? Justice?" he asked loudly.

"Sir?" the agent said to him again.

"Sorry about that," DJ replied. "I know you said not to speak directly to her."

"Officer Michaels, do you have your service weapon on you sir?" the agent asked.

"I do. It's in my back waste," he replied. "I can take it out or you can, whichever makes you comfortable," he added.

"I'll get it sir. Please remain still."

"Can I at least find out what I or Ms. Cooper are being taken in for questioning for?" he asked.

"Sure, I can answer that," the agent said.

DJ listened while he watched the female officer first check Justice for what, he didn't know and then the same officer opened the silver beaded purse that Justice had with her and search it thoroughly. He wondered what they were looking for.

"There are no charges, just yet, but you're both being taken in on conspiracy to commit fraud against the state of New York, burglary, theft, money-wiring fraud, prostitution, blackmailing a public official and so many more charges, I can't even get through them all before the sun comes up. You can find out about everything after we've taken her to FBI headquarters. You'll be there for questioning as well to see what you know about her criminal activity, but I understand that first, you're needed at the Center."

DJ was getting pissed off with all the secrecy and hearing what they are being taken in for was ludicrous. He hadn't broken any laws, and definitely not any of the things he'd just been told about. What bothered him the most was as he continued to look at Justice, she didn't seem to be as shocked as he was. He watched her shoulders slack as she now seemed to looked defeated. He was no longer looking at the strong, confident woman he'd come to fall in love with. She looked more like a perp that he'd picked up on many occasions who had finally been caught red-handed.

"So, we're not going in together?" DJ asked.

"No, sir. She'll go in one car and you'll be taken in another. We won't put cuffs on you, out of respect for you as an officer and because, frankly, I'm not so sure you're involved, but we know Ms. Cooper is. We've been investigating her and her friends for almost six months now and all I can tell you is that this goes far and wide and involves the Mayor, the commissioner and other top city government officials. Ms. Cooper is in a lot of trouble. Now, come with us and let's see if we can get this all sorted out. If you're involved in her schemes, she's just taken you down with her."

DJ didn't know what to say from what he was just told. He looked across the car at Justice as her arms were placed in front of her, instead of behind her while handcuffs were placed on her wrists. Still, her eyes avoided his.

He followed the officer's instructions and didn't say anything to Justice as she was led away from him. Until he could get more information about the situation, he would utilize his right to remain silent. There had to be some kind of a mistake.

"Once they are a little further away, I'll escort you to the Center. There is a room that'll I'll escort you to and hopefully, you'll be able to get some answers before I escort you to the FBI building. Bear with me a few more minutes," the agent said.

As the female agent led Justice away, DJ watched another go through his car. He didn't know what they were looking for, but he was sure they wouldn't find anything. After picking up his rental, he'd gone straight to pick up Justice and she'd only come out in her gown with her purse in her hand.

"This has got to be some kind of a mistake," he uttered as they finally began to walk away.

"She sure is beautiful and I'm telling you, if she scammed you into helping her, you aren't the first. Do you even know who she really is? I get the feeling the only one of the two of you who knows what's going on, is her. You are about to get the shock of your life. I knew she was beautiful from the photos we have of her, but I had no idea any woman could be that beautiful. I see how so many men could be taken in by her just by her looks. I also understand she's quite intelligent and carries herself with a lot of confidence. That can be a powerful took again vulnerable men," the agent said.

"You're saying I was vulnerable and caught up in something? If so, you're wrong on both accounts. This is all just a big mistake. You'll see, it's all a mistake," DJ said.

"Sir, from my vantage point, the only thing I'm not sure about is your involvement. As for her, she's in deep and you have no idea how far down the rabbit whole this goes. You are about to find out," agent said.

DJ watched the female officer walk a handcuffed Justice to a waiting federal car and even when she was placed inside with the doors closed and locked, she never looked his way, even when he walked by the car and tried to get her attention. He watched her purposely looked the opposite way from him.

"What just happened?" he uttered to himself. "What the hell is going on?" he said louder. Though no one responded, he knew he had been heard.

1

Chicago, Illinois
Present Day

DJ checked the time on his cell phone for the tenth time in the past five minutes as he lay atop the covers in his king-sized bed in the two-bedroom apartment that he'd found not long after his move back to Chicago after his life crashed and burned in New York. Not only did he have this apartment, but he loved the suite at the casino that Torrence, his soon to be brother-in-law, gave him to stay in when he worked long shifts as one of three guys who shared the role of head of security at the Chicago casino that was Torrence's pride and joy. He could never thank his sister Reese and Torrence enough for the new opportunity to do something with his life after coming back home. The scandal could have ruined his life, but it didn't and they were giving him an opportunity to get his life back on track and truth be told, he was happy to be back in Chicago where he was closer to his family, especially his mother, and his sisters, Reese and Nichelle.

As he lay in bed, still unable to shake the thought of Justice from his mind and what seeing her again could potentially do to his life, good and bad, he also thought of the outcome of what happened in New York which made the headline news where names were named with the exception of the name of a key contributor to it all, Justice Cooper. He now knew that she'd met him using an alias. Her real name was Avalon Hart and she was the sister of Jermony Jamison, one of the highest paid professional basketball players in the country. People put his game on the same level as Kobe Bryant and Lebron James. Jermony was a powerful figure and knew why Justice's name was nowhere in the news. He thought by now that she would be sweating life out behind bars. For an entire year, he checked the news and waited for word that she had been charged and convicted, but he got nothing. He soon discovered the entire situation had been swept under the rug and though great men had been taken down, Avalon had come out squeaky clean because she was out free and in Chicago, roaming around as if she didn't have a care in the world after fraud, conspiracy, theft and prostitution charges were somehow dropped. He never believed the prostitution part of the charges, but in checking with a few contacts, he found out that she wasn't actually doing anything like that herself, but she had a hand in hooking women up with other officers and so the charge was still levied against her.

After running into her a few days ago at the casino, he had been doing everything he could to avoid her. She'd been at the casino a few times since then and was told she'd been asking about him. To save face, he would send one of his officer's to see if she needed help with something casino related and the answer was always, no. He knew she was looking for him specifically and it had nothing to do with work. It wasn't that he didn't want to see her; he was concerned about what he would do being in her presence again. She was forbidden fruit because he knew how addicted to her he had been before and he didn't want to be in that position again. He didn't *want* her that much. He didn't *want* to be in love with her anymore. It's been a year and here he was embarrassed that he had been taken in and also angry that his heart and his body still desired her.

He and Diego had stayed in contact and it was his friend who told him there was a lot of jobs loss behind the scandal, but that it had all been done quietly. There was no hiding the names of the higher-ups, but even they had disappeared from the spotlight as if they never existed. The theft ring that Justice had been involved in was larger than anyone even thought. Since everything that was stolen had been recovered after all of the merchandise had been found at a storage facility and those who had been swindled refused to testify, no charges were ever filed against her or any others, to his surprise and dismay. With his anger, he wanted someone to pay, but other than the jobs lost, no one else suffered.

Avalon had been arrested right in front of him as they were heading to a high-profile event being thrown by the commissioner for the campaign of the Mayor who was running for re-election soon. While that event was taking place, the FBI closed in on all of those involved in a scheme that involved counterfeit money, high-class prostitutes and theft from houses of rich guests who were at the party while their houses were being robbed – something the FBI had known was happening. There were so many ups and downs to the case and so much of it was never even in the news, but he knew all about what happened until all knowledge of

Justice/Avalon ceased.

DJ had been angered by that consider he had been fired from the force, not for doing anything wrong, but for what the FBI and New York Police Department were unable to find out. Rather than fight it, he was more than ready to get out of New York anyway. He received a nice settlement, something he called hush money. He was happy his name was wiped clean during the investigation, but still, he had been linked to Avalon and that was enough for him to not fight being let go. Luckily, instead of his record stating he had been terminated, it stated that he had resigned. He welcomed it and with the help of his sister and Torrence, within a week, he was heading back home to Chicago where he was born and raised. He needed to be around people he loved and trusted.

DJ still needed to know what happened; what really happened. He got the police version, but he knew there was more to it and he deserved answers. Jermony had mentioned that he was able to get his sister away from the scandal, free and clear, and he had no doubt with the pull Jermony had and with the people he knew, that he was able to do just that. He still needed to know how and he intended to find out. On the tip of his tongue were the words that Avalon had ruined his life, but he couldn't say them because he'd allowed her to ruin his life by not keeping his eyes and ears as open as he had with his pants and his bed.

As Justice, she came into his life like a whirlwind, bringing fire and a zest for life he'd never experienced before with any woman. She was so alive, so unbothered, so confident, so affection and more uninhibited sexually than he'd ever experienced. He was far from being an angel when it came to bedding women. He'd had more than a few casual flings, most one-night-stands because he didn't want to get his heart involved, both before and after his last relationship that had led to an engagement with a woman he thought he saw forever with. In less than six months of meeting Justice, he'd fallen in love and had been duped again.

As he tossed around in his bed, DJ couldn't help but think back to his first date with Justice which was for dinner at one of his favorite deli shops after one of his shifts. He didn't venture out much since he worked until midnight on most nights, but when she agreed to meet him at midnight, he couldn't pass up the chance to see her again. For a week, they had talked through the night when he got off until either one of them would fall asleep while talking. Their talks were so blunt, open and, what he thought were honest, and he was immediately drawn into her love of life. He wasn't looking for anything serious and neither was she. He liked that she had made the first move by slipping him her number. When they finally met, he liked everything about her and to say that she was gorgeous would be an understatement.

Justice was twenty-five, five-foot-seven, with sexy long legs and on top of them rested the sexy behind and flat abs, which added to her coke bottle figure. At the deli that night, she wore a red button-down shirt tied at her waist with the buttons opened and underneath, she had on a V-neck t-shirt and encased in that shirt were large, round and from his imagination, firm breasts. Her long, natural two-toned hair in brown and blond twists were pulled up into a ponytail and her face was beyond beautiful. She had on light makeup and he loved that she realized she didn't need much because her beauty was all-natural. He could tell by the way she was dressed and her perfectly manicured nails and freshly done hair that she loved taking care of herself. When she opened her mouth to talk, the soft, yet smoky sound of her voice was magnetic. It wasn't high-pitched, but instead, deep and melodious, the way he imagined T-Boz from TLC would sound in a conversation based on the sound of her voice when she sang. He didn't care how old T-Boz got or if she never sang again, she would forever be his favorite songstress by how enticing the sound of her voice was. Justice had that same tone to her voice and he longed for her to say more and more throughout that night and every night after that first date.

They sat in the diner that night until the middle of the night talking about everything just to keep their time together from ending. He really thought she was instantly into him as he was into her. As their time together was winding down, he'd done something he had never done before. Justice invited herself home with him and he took her up on that offer. They had spent the evening flirty non-stop and she was irresistible. She looked at him across the table with her beautiful eyes in a shade of light brown that he'd never seen before. He had even asked if she had on contacts and she assured him, her hazel eyes were real. She got them from her mother, who was white and not from her father who was African American. Her look was exotic and one look from her was all it took for him to fall under her spell.

Since he wasn't in his patrol car, avoiding risking another unofficial ride for her in it, he paid the check and they walked to his car, a navy blue Mustang.

In New York, he lived in a small brownstone, two-floor

apartment out in New Rochelle, New York. He knew the ins and outs of getting around and in no time, they were at his place. Once inside, he offered her a bottle of water and after taking one sip, she told him she didn't come home with him for water. She drew him in even more to her web by telling him that from the moment she saw him, she was interested in what was under his uniform.

At thirty, DJ knew that he'd met a lot of bold women in his time, but none as bold as she was. He had a sister her age and didn't like the idea that his sister would be this bold with men. He couldn't think about that because the only thoughts on his mind were of Justice, especially when she removed her red shirt and turned to him with her hands on her hips as if she was waiting impatiently on him.

DJ remembered how on fire his body was, much like it is now as he lay in bed, thinking about their first encounter – an explosive night. Even now, when he reached down his body, his rock hard penis was a reminder that all it took was one thought of her and his body was in desperate need of her touch. The things she knew how to do when it came to pleasing him was beyond his wildest desires. He had locked eyes with her and they stood like that for what seemed an eternity with his pulse quickening and his heart racing at the sheer level of desire he felt for her, after only meeting her twice in person. He wanted her with a fierceness that his body had never exhibited before, but first he wanted to make sure she understood his rules; he wasn't looking for a relationship. When he shared that with her, she told him to shut up and kiss her and he did or he thought he was when in fact, the moment his lips touched hers, he lost all train of thought and he knew she was in control of the stimulating kiss.

His mind had gone blank as her lips worked him over. Her kiss was hot and passionate and full of need and want that he just went with it. Clothes starting flying all over the place and before they could even get to a bed, he quickly went in search of a condom and raced back to pick her up. Within seconds, he was inside of her up against the wall with her legs wrapped tight around his waist. Their copulation was something out of an X-rated movie. Sex that night had been wild, uninhibited and out of control and the best he'd ever had. He thought he was bringing his best game and yet, she had put something on him. Her mouth was electric, her hands were everywhere. Her moans and mewling drove him on to give her more and more and when his lips and tongue laved her, and she came apart in his arms again and again, he knew he had finally met his match sexually. They had orgasmed so many times that night that he'd actually lost count. That morning before she left, they went at it again in the shower and he loved her excited use of his shower gel. From that first encounter, they had a hard time keeping their hands off of each other. Even now, images of her played with his head as his body hardened even more with remembrance of their time together.

Avalon, as Justice back then, was the kind of woman he could find himself actually getting serious about. He'd introduced her to the few friends he'd made in New York. They had even double-dated with Diego and his wife, Aryah. He saw no signs back then that something was going on, but now when he thought back to those five or so months they spent together, there were a lot of red flags.

Justice had kept her personal life close to her. When he

asked about family or close friends, she only spoke of her two roommates. She never wanted to talk about her family or where she was originally from. He wanted to know, but he didn't pry because at that time, they were only having fun. There were times when she would disappear or take secret phone calls and biggest of all, she would ask a lot of questions about his life on the force, often asking about specific officers. Once, he had caught her doing, what he felt was flirting between her and the police commissioner at a pickup basketball game which was a fundraiser for local boys and girls clubs, but she explained it as her being excited to meet the top cop in passing. What he later found out after everything went down was that the commissioner was a client of one of her roommates who made a living servicing powerful men.

DJ had been left wondering if she had been doing the same thing once he found out about the who scheme, but then brushed that off. He may not know some things about her, but that, he was sure of. After things crashed and burned, he never got the chance to speak to her again. He was questioned for days about what he knew and he had been telling the truth when he said he didn't know anything at all. He had been blindsided to know that she had so much going on behind his back and practically in front of his face.

Now that she was in Chicago, he had a lot of questions and if she owed him anything for what she took him through and for how his life was turned upside down, she owed him an explanation of what happened back then and he was planning on getting it. He didn't care that Jermony warned him to stay away from her. He didn't fear Jermony as much as he feared the unknown.

Seeing her the other night reminded him that except for a few one-night-stands since returning to Chicago, he had not let another woman get close to him because he was on guard. He had allowed Justice to slip through his defenses and that had led to his embarrassing removal from the force. He didn't think about applying for a position with the police force in Chicago and when Torrence told him he had all the trust and faith in him in the world to run the security force at the casino, he took him up on his offer and the job paid much more than what he was making as a police officer. He had been trying to take his life in a better direction only to be sidetracked when she showed up. He needed to get used to the fact that Justice was not her real name. She was Avalon Hart and any way he looked at it, even though she was the hottest woman he'd ever met, she had swindled him in ways he still didn't understand how without him knowing. He hated himself for being blind to her antics, but he wasn't done with her yet. No one got over on him that way. He was nicknamed Black, yes for the fact that he always wore black, but also because his personality was dark and mysterious, though his skin was light, bright and damn near white. The darkness he considered his life to be was out of unhappiness over his childhood.

His life wasn't the best because he had a father who only cared about the next woman and not about the wife and kids he had at home. DJ had to seek out male role models from other men and even if his father had been around, he wouldn't want him as a model. His sisters Nichelle and Reese, had, over time, built up a relationship with their father, but he still struggled with forgiving him for his past deeds. Now, here he was with another person that had let him down and he wished it didn't bother him as much as it did.

He had tried keeping things with Avalon as casual as possible, but in the end, right before his world tumbled out of control back in New York, he'd fallen in love with her. He had lost himself in her without giving it a second thought. She appeared in his life suddenly and had disappeared just as fast. What bothered him the most was the fact that the minute he saw her at the casino, he pretty much forgot that she'd destroyed his life. He saw that sexy, beautiful woman he loved having in his arms and making love to night after night. This was a woman he thought cared about him like no woman ever had before. She was interested in his day and now he knew why. She was affectionate all the time and whenever he reached for her with desirous thoughts, her thoughts and desires matched his. She cooked for him, he cooked for her, and they cooked together. They were building a life he didn't realize they were building because his feelings for her crept up on him only to be shattered the night of the gala event. How could he still be attracted to her?

"Easy," he said out loud to himself. *"She's fine as hell!"* he added and then reached for the bulge that had formed in his boxers, even harder now than a few minutes ago. He closed his eyes and thought about her and the way her hand seductively caressed his manhood at the casino in front of the elevator, causing the usual reaction he would have to her and for that, he hated himself. He didn't know any better than to stay away from her and not want her. *"Damn!"* he yelled out of frustration at himself as he looked down his body and knew he was a lost cause. Just the idea of her had him hard as a rock. Being without her, kissing her, making love to her all these months was having a drastic impact on him. He still wanted her fiercely.

His ringing phone jarred him back to reality and not to that world where he was still thinking of making a fool of himself for another sexy night with her.

When he saw his sister Reese calling, he turned his thoughts away from Avalon and sat up on the side of his bed, cleared his throat in hopes that he could also clear his mind.

"Hey Sis!" he said, making his voice sound cheerful.

"Hey back to you. What happened last night? I was expecting you at Mommy's house for dinner? Nichelle and I tried calling and your cell went to voicemail all night. I'm surprised you answered now," Reese said.

DJ didn't want to admit that once he'd gotten home from the casino, not wanting to bunk in his room there for the night, he'd come home, turned off his phone in hopes to tune out the world. He forgot about stopping at his mother's house and so he lied.

"I hadn't powered it up and when it lost power, I meant to turn it on as soon as it had a little juice and I forgot until sometime in the middle of the night when I did turn it on. What did I miss with the family gathering?" he asked.

"Not much. Just your baby sister acting all weird and stuff. Mommy is seeing this guy and you need to meet him. I know you've been back for a while and every time David's name comes up, you come up with a new excuse for not meeting him. What's up with that?" Reese asked.

As the oldest of them, Reese was always trying to patch up all of their lives, especially their mother's. He knew about this great guy his mother was seeing who owned some kind of golf resort or country club or something, but he wasn't ready to meet any man his mother was seeing. He still had images of the horrible way his father treated their mother and he didn't want her with any man if the possibility arose that he could mistreat her. He wasn't sure he would be able to control his anger if that was the case. With Reese as the oldest, she took on the role of always being in control and he let her, but he also knew how persistent she can be when things don't go her way and him missing another family dinner was her not getting her way and he knew he was about to hear it.

"Don't you have your own love live to be all invested in? How are things with you and Torrence? The wedding still on? I know how you can be all wishy-washy when it comes to your own personal life. Things better now that you're engaged and all? No more side chicks for Torrence? Tell him to throw one or two my way!" DJ joked and knew that now that Reese's love life was back on track after Torrence's admission that he had been cheating on her with several women including one who went ballistic when she came to Chicago from Dubai to claim her man. They could all laugh about it now, but he knew it was a hard time for her when she'd fallen in love for the first time in her life only to find out that Torrence was all swagger with a lot of baggage that followed him into her life.

"He better not if he knows what's good for him. We're good and I'm looking forward to getting married. I wanted to talk to you about that last night too along with what's up with you and Jermony's sister. The wedding first. We need to talk about daddy and the wedding and I don't want to do it over the phone," Reese said.

DJ stood up suddenly and grabbed his head with his

hand when an instant headache tried to surface. Any discussions about his father did that to him.

"Can we not do it today? I have enough on my mind and talking about him will only mess up my day," he said.

"I know, baby brother, but we have to do it. It's my wedding and I want my family there – *all* of my family. We can talk when you're ready. The wedding is now still some time away and yes, we changed the date again. You know Torrence is working on plans to build another casino, his third besides the one in Vegas and the one here in Chicago and we are crazy busy with that. The good thing is, the wedding will be at the casino here in Chicago, so that will save lots of money and time on my original plan for a destination wedding," she said.

"*Money?* Girl, you are not worried about money. Your man is loaded and you're not doing bad either with your own marketing firm now that you've decided to partner with your old firm to lead all of their marketing as a subcontractor. I hear that contract is fat with them is huge; mega bucks and that doesn't even include your own clients. Didn't you just hire for new managers and ten or so new staff? I'm trying to live large like you one day," DJ exclaimed.

"Yeah, well, I'm hoping to see you in love one day and not worried about living large. I want you to live happy. Do you want to tell me about Jermony's sister and how you're connected to her? That scene at the casino only gave me surface information, but I need more. Sienna and I were talking about that yesterday. What's this about Jermony getting her out of some scandal in New York that included you? You still haven't told me much about what happened in New York. I know you've told Torrence because you've gotten close to him as a brother and I like that you have him to connect with, but I'm your big sister and I want you to connect with me too," Reese said.

DJ could imagine Reese on the other end of the phone pouting as she was known to do when she felt left out. Seeing her and all of her facial moods is something he missed while living in New York.

"You and me have no problem with communication. We connect all the time and you know it. That time in my life was embarrassing and I'm not ready to talk about it yet, but I promise you, when I think the time is right, I will fill you in. Just don't tell mommy or Nicki about any of this, okay?" he asked.

"I got you," Reese affirmed.

"How did you come to know Jermony? I know of him, but I don't know him as well as you and your friends do. He recently found out Avalon was his sister?" he asked.

"I met Jermony back in college. He's best friends with Carter and Sienna. For a short stint, Carter played college basketball, which is where he and Jermony got closer. He also knew him from the old neighborhood. The one thing about Carter is he did a good job of befriending guys who could use a father figure, like Dexter and Jermony who were fatherless. Carter's mother and father would invite Carter's friends to come home from college on breaks like Thanksgiving and Christmas, especially those who didn't have much family and Jermony was one of those guys. Carter's parents treated him like a son just like they did with Dexter. Jermony found out that his father was a rolling stone and had children in several area codes. He put a private eye in place to track them down about a year or so ago and he's making some progress. His first find was Avalon. He calls her Avie. He never had much of a family and now that he has a family of his own, he wants to connect his kids to any family he can find. That's how he was able to find Avalon. I think he said his father had seven or eight kids, something he found out from an aunt on his mother's side of the family. I don't know much else about it, but if you ask Torrence, he might know or even ask Carter. Better yet, ask Jermony. I hear the two of you sort of bumped heads over his sister, but he's really a cool guy. He's already over-protective of her, so tread lightly. You were involved with her? Is that it?" Reese asked.

DJ exhaled loudly as he walked around, wearing a hole in the plush navy-blue carpet that covered his bedroom floor. He didn't want to get into much about Avalon.

"I was and it was a mistake. I mean, it was the biggest mistake of my life," he said.

"That may be the case, but I also remember a particular conversation with you about her, but you called her Justice back then. You called me on the phone and told me you were falling in love with a woman named Justice and you wanted me to meet her. We talked about how your previous engagement hadn't turned out well, but you were really into this woman. Justice and Avalon are the same person, right?" she inquired.

"Yes, but I didn't know her name was Avalon. She was going by Justice when she lived in New York. Again, a very long story I can't get into right now, but I will at some point. I need to get moving. I have to get to the casino. The other security managers from the other shifts are coming in for a meeting so that we can start talking about security for the campaign fundraiser for City Council President Tucker Glass."

"Oh, he's a cool dude. He's a friend of Carter's," she said.

"From school?" DJ asked.

"No. They are on the board together for the boys and girls club of Chicago and Carter runs a mentorship program and partners with other powerful African American men to allow boys and young men from the city to shadow them and Tucker has been hailed as one of the biggest supporters of the program. He has had several young men shadow him at City Hall and a few are looking to go into politics because of him."

"Cool. Torrence told the staff about the fundraiser and how he's planning to go all out for the event. He wants to be sure we have our full security team in place that night, though Tucker is coming with his own security as well."

"I notice you changed the subject of disappearing on us last night, but I'll let that slide for now because I know you have a lot going on. Keep your head in the game, okay? Watch your back and if you can, keep your mind off of Avalon. I saw how the two of you looked at each other. I saw you at the elevator together and don't worry, no one saw but me. The heat between the two of you is obvious and if we weren't in a public place, you would have devoured each other. The fire between the two of you is hot and we could all sense it. Whatever happened between you, figure it out and then stay on top of the job."

DJ knew she was right. He only hoped he could follow her instruction. He couldn't lose another job because of the same woman.

"I know, sis. I'm thankful Torrence has given me this

opportunity and I love the job. It's a lot of hours and a lot to oversee, but I got it covered and I won't get distracted this time. How many times do I have to tell you to always bet on *Black* to get the job done! I got this. I'll call you later and I promise to make the next family dinner," DJ said.

"Good, because it's in three days on Sunday and it's at my house, so be there or we're going to all come to your place and you know how much Mommy is looking forward to get to your place to redecorate it. I'm protecting you, so don't screw me over by missing another dinner. Got it?" Reese shouted into the phone.

DJ laughed and shook his head as if she could see him.

"Yeah, I got it. I'll be there. I'll call mom in a bit and apologize and what's up with Nichelle?" he asked.

"Oh, we'll talk about that. She was acting all secretive last night and lately she's been dressing differently. Not different bad, but different good. You know she was into the bohemian look, no real pomp and circumstance. Now, she's wearing make-up, her hair is always perfect, her nails and toes are polished with designs and last night, she had on high-heeled, sexy shoes with the hottest red, casual dress on. I'm just wondering why the sudden change," Reese questioned. "I think she was going out on a date with a man after dinner. Remember I told you she was trying to figure out her sexuality. One day, about a year ago, she told me she was something called fluid. She wouldn't even explain it to me. She said look it up. I did and it gave me a better understanding. You know I've always been here for both of you and I know she was experimenting with her sexuality. I think there is a guy, now, and whoever he is, I think it's getting serious. I was going to ask her about it, but decided to mind my business until she comes to me needing to talk. I'm worried about her," Reese explained.

"Don't sweat it. She's fine. As long as no one is hurting her or using her, let her have her space. If she needs us, she'll come to you or me based on what's going on. If this dude hurts her, she better come to you first because if it's me, I'm going to be all over him. You know how I am when it comes to her. She's the youngest and not as strong as you are. Don't worry so much, mother hen," he joked. "Call you later?" DJ asked.

"Yup, I'll be around. I'll stop by the office when I get to the casino later. Love you, Black," Reese said.

DJ smiled. Most people called him either Black or DJ and Reese used both. He answers to both – just not when anyone calls him Delvin, well, except Avalon. She said his name like it was the best thing since popcorn and it sounded that way to his ears.

"Love you more," he said, hanging up and running to the shower.

The minute he removed his gray sweat pants and jumped in the shower and grabbed the shower gel, his thoughts once again turned to Avalon and the things she did with her hands and his shower gel. Instantly, his body hardened and a certain part of his body stood at attention when a picture of her down on her knees in front of him, working him over with her hands and that gel. Turning the water from hot to ice cold, he tried to think of something other than all of her lusciousness and hoped that he could resist her because his body was fighting a losing battle and his mind and heart were slowly following.

2

Avalon kicked off her shoes and stretched her legs out on the large brown leather sectional in one of the three family rooms in Jermony's large seventeen thousand square foot house. The place was bigger than any house she'd ever been in, not that she ever really had the opportunity present itself for her to be in a house this big before now. She still couldn't believe her luck that her brother was a famous professional basketball player, richer than any person she ever knew. His house was actually the same size as the house that Sean "Diddy" Combs lived in out in Los Angeles and that's saying something.

The house boasted nine garage bays, eleven bedrooms and sixteen bathrooms, three family rooms, three kitchens, indoor and outdoor swimming pools, two basketball courts, one indoor and one outdoor court, tennis court, an in-home gym, complete with a sauna and massage room, with full staff in place during the times when he would be home and, so much more. Her brother was living *thee* life. There was so much to see that she was exhausted from the first mini tour he'd given her when she first arrived in Chicago three months ago. At first, she was pretty low-key until that event at the casino where she went as his guest when his wife decided not to go. She was excited about being able to splurge on her look for the night. Being in Chicago was good for her and she was glad that she finally decided to move even though she didn't have much of a choice. She needed a clean slate and Chicago was it.

After going through the drama in New York, she didn't originally accept his offer for her to come stay with him and his family in Chicago. She was hesitant, not understanding how to accept an offer of help from someone who was now family.

When she was first approached about the possibility that she had a brother who was looking for her, but that she couldn't yet find out who he was, she went along with the request to have a blood test done to find out if they were related. She didn't see the harm and if it turned out to be true, she would have someone else in the world besides the woman she called her mother, whom she believed never cared about her from the moment she'd given birth to her. The fact that her mother never had any other children led her to believe that she never wanted to have any children to begin with and still couldn't figure out why she actually went through with having her.

From as far back as she could remember as a child, her mother had been horrible to her and she shuddered at the thought of the awful and demeaning things her mother made her do as a child and as a teenager until the day she couldn't take it anymore. When she knew her mother was on the brink of throwing her out of the house, she packed what she could fit into a back pack and she left. That wasn't the extent of what happened, but with her unwillingness to go along with her mother's diabolical mind, she knew getting thrown out was coming. She wished she could say that was the end of her interaction with her mother, but it wasn't. Virginia Hart or Ginny, as she preferred to be called, even over being called mom or mother, was never meant to be a mother, but for the life of her, Avalon couldn't seem to break completely free of her.

Even after leaving home at the age of fifteen, her mother, though she didn't want her to come back home, still kept tabs on her and demanded total obedience from her only child. When she heard she could possibly have a brother who was looking for her, the idea brought an excitement to her life that she'd never had before. She knew that the man who got her mother pregnant had a lot of other children according to her mother, but she knew nothing about him. She didn't know who he was, but she didn't care. She loved the idea that there was someone else out in the world that she could possibly finally call family.

Her mother hated her own family and Avalon never met any of them. From what she knew of her father, he had been married when he hooked up with her mother and as long as it was just the two of them messing around, he was fine, but when her mother turned up pregnant, her father did what he was known to do; disappear. She knew his name, but not much about him. His name was so common that even if she tried to find him, it would have been hard and she wouldn't know where to start.

She was told by the private investigator who approached her that the mysterious, possible brother of hers had tracked her down through family of his who remembered who her mother was. She agreed to the blood test and when the results came back and she found out who her brother was, she was ecstatic. At that time, she was in the middle of a scheme to make herself more money and had involved some pretty important people in New York. Knowing she had a rich brother didn't discourage her from going through with the plans already in place and when she was caught, the first thing she did was call Jermony and he came through and took care of everything. After that, she didn't stay in New York; she couldn't. Though her brother was able to get the slate wiped clean as far as her not having a record, the FBI made it clear that she needed to make her home someplace else other than in New York. She decided on Maryland, for no real reason. She was a wanderer so a new place was nothing for her. Jermony gave her money to get a place of her own and she headed south. For a few months, that worked and then she got bored. She didn't really miss New York or any part of her old life, but she did miss DJ. He was the happiness she never thought she'd find, but the timing wasn't great.

After Maryland got old after a few months, she called Jermony and asked if she could join him in Chicago. He was on the road at an away game, but he sent a private jet to pick her up at the airport.

The original plan was for her to stay with him at his mansion, but his wife, Kimberly, had other plans. She didn't trust as easily as Jermony did and rather than be uncomfortable, especially with Jermony gone most of the time traveling on the road with his basketball team, she didn't want to feel like she wasn't wanted. She'd had enough of that all her life with her own mother. Jermony arranged for her to have a large suite at a five-star hotel until she decided what she wanted to do. He had even gotten her a room a time or two at the casino, which she loved. If she decided to stay in Chicago, Jermony offered to buy her a place, get her a car and help her get on her feet until she figured out what she wanted to do with her life. She was still figuring that out. All she knew was how to hustle people to get by and Jermony was constantly reminding her that she no longer had to do that. A friend of his had recently offered to let her move into an apartment that his girlfriend had moved out of, leaving several months on her lease. She was all set to do that because the last thing she wanted was bad blood between her and her brother's wife. What she still needed to figure out was the chances of running into DJ again after a year. He still looked at hot and sexy as he had when they were together. She missed him and even more so after seeing him a few nights ago. She'd tried to connect with him since then by going back to the casino a few times and asking for him, but she was getting the feeling that he was purposely avoiding her, something that pissed her off. There was no doubt he still wanted her and her desire for him was unmeasurable. She'd gone back to her hotel that night and the way she pleasured herself thinking about him had her body quaking again and again. Even before that night, she couldn't imagine letting another man touch her and when she touched herself, it was his face that she saw. It was images of his body in her head that turned her on. She missed him and even knowing she had no right to after what she did, she still did.

Even now, she thought back on her life in New York and how it had all gone so wrong. Thoughts of DJ entered her mind and every time she thought of him, she was reminded of how much she hurt the one man who ever really cared about her. What kind of person drags a man down into her piss-pool of a life when all he wanted to do was care for her?

DJ had been devastated when he found out what she had been doing and, in some part, she had used him to get it done. She never got the chance to explain anything to him and even if she could, she didn't know what she would have said. She played it off when she saw him at the casino, resorting to her usual playful, salacious self, but inside, she was embarrassed and hoped that he had it within himself to forgive her. How do you tell a man who cared so much for you that meeting him was not a coincidence and that she'd set it up for them to meet that night? She was the saddest of people. She had no idea the kind of wonderful man DJ was until after she had a chance to know him. She'd run game on men before because she had to in order to survive being on her own at a young age. She'd gotten herself hooked up to some powerful men in New York and one of those was DJ's captain. His captain had told her where DJ would be and that if she worked her usual charm and got close to him, she would be able to get closer to the commissioner who had become fond of DJ after he spent some time on the security detail for the top cop. The captain was in on the money scheme and since he couldn't be seen with her, he wanted to still keep her close enough to the inside to allow her to work her magic and work them all is what she'd done. The plan was not good enough because in the end, the FBI was already onto the scheme and she'd been caught.

New York flashed in her head and for as long as she lived, she would never forget that time, especially the last night she'd been with DJ. They were in the car together and happy. She was genuinely happy.

That night, the FBI agents had flooded the city and were actually arresting all those involved as they arrived for the gala that she'd been looking forward to going to with DJ for weeks. She knew he would ask her to go with him and that was the night that the scheme would finally be put to action. With all the dignitaries at the event, their houses would be prime for the taking and there were scores of people in place to enter those houses and rob them of everything valuable, but it didn't turn out that way. She knew that the owners would file insurance claims, but would never publicly acknowledge the theft. There was too much dirt on all of them with young women, since most were married and wouldn't want that information to get out. Instead, a few had quietly gone to jail, well federal prison, which was better than most people's homes. Some also disappeared after not being charged, but given the option to retire from the force and live their lives elsewhere. There were a lot of divorces from women who were sick and tired of their cheating husbands. Bigger than the money scheme was the money a lot of men spent on women, some she even helped supply. Nothing had happened to her, thanks to Jermony. Now, she was in Chicago and because of her mother's threats, she was thinking of a new scam, this time to possibly include the casino. Her mother would not let go and wherever she went, her mother would find her and issue threats that made her conform to her whims. When she told Ginny about the casino, her next question was how she was going to get rich by Avalon ripping it off. What her mother didn't know was that the man whom she'd been unable to forget about was head of security at the casino she'd heard a lot about. She was trying to think of a plan that wouldn't involve DJ. She couldn't hurt him like that again.

Her plan was to get close to some of the men working the tables and work them over to get chips to cash in and give her mother the money she was blackmailing her for. If she didn't get money that way, her mother expected her to get it from Jermony by any means necessary and the amount was no small amount. Jermony would never give her that amount of money and she wouldn't dare tell him what her mother had on her that would cause her to get back into the street-hustling life. She didn't see a way out, but as long as her mother was still in North Carolina where she'd left her, she could buy herself some time and figure a way out of her newest jam.

"Comfy?"

Avalon turned and placed her feet on the floor when Jermony entered the family room.

"Sorry. I was going to watch some television. Should I not have my feet up on the seat? I promise they're clean," she said, brushing off imaginary dust from the seat cushion as Jermony came around and sat at the opposite end of the sectional.

"You're fine. I'm just picking with you. It's a family room and you can get as comfortable as you want. You should see this room after the kids spend a few hours in here. It will look like a tornado tore through it," he joked. "What are you watching?" he asked.

Avalon picked up the remote, turned the sound up and clicked to see what she was watching. She didn't know because she was preoccupied with her head filled with her own drama.

"Some comedy special. I was looking for the one with Dave Chappell that I heard was really good," she said, pressing the button and going from chancel to channel.

"I saw his latest and it was good. Some people were offended by it, but it was all about making people laugh and sometimes, you have to laugh at yourself, especially in this crazy world. Hand me the remote, I'll find it for you," Jermony said.

Avalon passed it to him and turned her body around to face the television.

"I love this room and I've never seen a television this big before. Do you spend a lot of time in this room? I know you have two other big rooms," she asked.

"When I'm home and looking to relax, I come in this room. One of the other two family rooms is filled with toys, which is where the kids hang out most of the time or I hang out with them there. This room is off limits to them when I'm home to keep one space in this house that I can come into and relax in quiet, especially after a bad game," he said.

"I hear things aren't going so well with your team making the playoffs," Avalon said.

"True. So much has been riding on these games, but we're the underdogs this year and that's cool. We're doing our best."

"What are you doing home in the middle of playoffs?" she asked.

"You know about basketball?" Jermony asked.

"Not much, but I heard you talking about it with Kimberly before you left the other day right after the event at the casino. I was surprised to get a text that you were home and you wanted to see me. Is something wrong? Did I do something?" Avalon asked cautiously.

She was still nervous from the moment she got his text saying he would be home for one day and wanted her to come out to the house to talk. On the ride over, she wondered if he was going to tell her that he changed his mind about wanting to be a part of her life. She'd never felt wanted by anyone other than him and DJ and after what she did to DJ, she didn't think he'd ever want to be near her again.

She did think that way until she encountered him at the casino and his immediate reaction to seeing her was just as it had been before she'd been arrested. He still wanted her and though their history wasn't the best, she still wanted him. She thought of nothing else but him since seeing him at the casino. She hoped he'd come find her on the casino floor any of the past few days that she'd gone back. She had done so to specifically search him out, but if he was there, he was avoiding her. She didn't blame him especially after she had time to think about how strongly she'd come on to him the other night as if nothing had gone on between them back in New York. She was surprised to see him and her body remembered what it was like to be loved by him all night long. When she saw signs of his desire for her rising, she couldn't help herself. She did what came naturally to her and she tried to smile through the look of disgust she saw on his face. He was still hurt and probably couldn't believe she would even think to touch him again. Until she saw him, she didn't realize how much she missed him.

"Avie?"

Avalon jumped at the sound of her nickname being

called. She didn't realize her mind had drifted off elsewhere.

"Oh, sorry. What did you say?" she asked.

"I said, you didn't do anything wrong. I haven't had a chance to talk to you since the event at the casino and I wanted to know about that interaction with Reese's brother, Black. What was that all about and why was he so aggressive and angry at you?" Jermony asked.

"You call him, Black?"

"Some call him DJ and others call him Black. I was told he prefers that name. I mean, I haven't had a lot of interaction with him, at least not directly. When I met him years ago, I remember his sister saying he likes to be called Black and I was reminded of that at the casino the other night. That's how he was introduced to me and I've been rolling with that. What was going on the other night? You knew him in New York? I heard him call you Justice. I thought that was all behind you," Jermony inquired.

"It is. I promise you it is, but to him, that's all he knew me as. We were involved when I was in New York and things had gotten pretty steamy between us before all hell broke loose. He was caught up in it through no fault of his own. I used him and that was before I really knew him and came to like him. I know you told him to stay away from me, but I wish you wouldn't have done that. I need to talk to him and explain what happened. I should be in prison and he knows that," she explained.

"Let's not go there. I was not going to let them lock you up. I was just getting to know my little sister and I went through too much to find you. Bottom line is, the powers that be trusted that I would get you on the right path and I intend to do that. You need to figure out what that right path is for you. If you and Black were involved in New York when that scandal broke, I don't think you should be involved now, but it's your life to live, not mine. How did he get caught up in it? Was he really not involved at all in what happened? I still don't understand it all."

Avalon shifted on the chair and tucked her feet under her.

"I know you want more answers and I promise to give them to you. I just can't visit all that again right now. I'm turning over a new leaf and trying to find my footing without bringing up the past again and again. I appreciate you helping me out and getting me out of trouble and I know I owe you," she said.

"Whoa – you don't *OWE* me anything. That's not what family does. I helped you because you're my sister and I'd help you again and again. I want you to be safe and happy and definitely not behind bars. Look, I don't want to bring up bad memories for you. All I ask is that you leave that life behind. You no longer have to hustle hard to survive. I am here to help you get on your feet. I want to help you get established and I even talked Torrence into giving you a shot at an office position at the casino administrative office. I spoke to him while I was away and he came through," Jermony admitted.

Avalon looked at him in shock and inwardly in horror, the last look she didn't want him to see.

"What? I was hoping to work on the casino floor," she said.

Avalon tried to not seem disappointed or ungrateful, but she had a different plan in mind.

"On the floor? I don't think you're ready for that kind of

temptation and Torrence knows a little about what happened in New York and not telling him some of what you have been through was not going to work if I was going to get his help. You said you wanted an honest job and I'm trying to help you get one. If he can make that work, give it a try," Jermony suggested.

Avalon smiled and kicked herself for not being as appreciative as she should be. Jermony was doing everything real family should do and she was questioning it. She would be in jail if it wasn't for Jermony finding her and then helping her. He didn't have to do anything for her. He really cared about her.

"Why did you look for me? I mean, why now? Are you still looking for the rest of our brothers and sisters?" she asked, changing the subject.

She watched the play of emotions that crossed Jermony's face as he leaned back and planted his feet wide in front of him.

"I lost my mother to breast cancer a few years ago and she was all I had as far as family that I was close to besides Kimberly and the kids. I had a younger brother who died in a swimming accident when him and some friends broke into a local gym and went swimming while they were drunk. He was fifteen at the time and I was seventeen. My father, or our father, left us after he and my mother had another one of their big blowout fights over his love for other women. She knew of the women and the out of wedlock children, but she'd finally had enough. From what I've been told, there are quite a few of us, that people remember. They remembered your mother, which is how I was able to track you down. We didn't actually reach out to her, but the private investigator I had was very thorough and he searched until he found you. We also have a little, little brother who is around five years old and yes, our father was still out here making babies five years ago. He's somewhere in the foster care system. So far, I haven't been able to locate him. His mother was a drug addict and surrendered him but no one knows where. It's possible, she was living in Arizona at the time. There are at least six maybe as many as eight other kids. You were the easiest to track down because everyone remembers your mother and the wild parties she would have which, from what I'm told, ended in sex-capades with our father. You were her only child?" he asked.

"Yeah. I was the only one she decided to have, though there were others that were conceived, but she got rid of. I remember being about thirteen and telling her that abortion is not to be used as a method for birth control. She'd done it so many times. She never wanted any other kids and to tell you the truth, she never really wanted me. She tells me all the time that she only wanted my dad, but that he didn't really want her – he only wanted her to be available to him when he wanted. After she got pregnant and he wanted nothing to do with her after she wouldn't have an abortion, she took me and left Chicago when I was a few months old. She thought he would come after her, but he never did. She once told me that she put his name on my birth certificate in case one day he came looking for us, but he never did. She never saw him again. I guess he moved on to the next mistress," Avalon said.

"He was definitely out there spreading his happy juice all over the place," Jermony joked.

"Is he still alive? Do you see him? His name is so

common, I never would have found him," she said.

For years, she wanted to know who her father was, but her mother was closed lipped about anything other than his name and it was so common that looking for him was like looking for a needle in a haystack.

"Right. Trying to find the right James Johnson was not going to be easy," Jermony quipped. "He's around someplace, but it's been years since I've seen or heard from him. I thought he would resurface with my career, but he hasn't. He may not be alive, but I wouldn't know. He's not on my list of people I want to find," he added.

"Thanks for looking for me and I'm really sorry if I compromised your life by throwing your name around in New York with the FBI. I didn't mean to cause you any grief," she said somberly, looking down at the floor in embarrassment.

"Don't sweat it, but don't keep doing that. Luckily the director of the FBI is a season ticket holder and loves Chicago basketball. He had my back, but I can't go back to that well a second time and ask for a favor as big as the one I asked for when it came to getting you out of that mess. I still think you should stay away from Black or DJ, whatever you call him. That could be trouble and you don't need that and I don't want to have to bail you out again," he said.

"Yeah, once was more than enough."

Avalon and Jermony turned when Kimberly walked into the room. What wasn't lost on Avalon was the look of annoyance on Kimberly's face and the look was directed at her. From the moment she met Kimberly, there was immediate bad blood and Avalon tried to avoid her at all cost. She knew Kimberly only tolerated her because of her love for Jermony, but the look of distrust was always on her face.

"Don't start Kimberly. Where are the kids?" Jermony asked.

"Swimming lessons. My mom just got here and is with them while I get laundry done," she explained.

"You do your own laundry?" Avalon asked, trying to lighten the mood.

When Kimberly whipped her long hair around at her as if the question was ridiculous.

"I do and I also cook and clean myself too," Kimberly answered.

"Wow. If I was in your shoes, I would never lift a finger to do anything. I would have people waiting on me around the clock," Avalon admitted selfishly.

"That's why I'm me and you're you. Are you staying for dinner? Jermony, you need to get ready for your flight. I told you not to come home for only a few hours. You don't want to be tired for your game with all this flying back and forth. I packed your bag and it's on the bed," Kimberly said.

"Thanks, babe. I wanted to see you guys and chat with Avalon before I hit the road. If we win this next game, we have a slim chance of advancing which means I'll be gone even longer on the road and I needed my family time. I'm going to hang around until sometime after the kids' lessons so that I can spend a little more time with them."

"Avalon? Dinner?" Kimberly asked abrasively, not hiding her dislike for her.

"Uh, no. I'm going to head out to go back to the hotel and relax. I was thinking of going to the casino for a few hours and then to a night club," she said.

"No job yet?" Kimberly asked.

"Kim! Seriously?" Jermony interjected.

Avalon watched Jermony stand up and walk around to where Kimberly stood.

"I was just asking," Kimberly blurted out.

"It's okay. No, I don't have a job yet. Jermony just told me that a friend of his may have an office job for me which I'm looking forward to," she lied.

"That hotel you're in is pretty expensive. A job could help you find a nice apartment to live in," Kimberly added.

"Actually, I found a place for her so she can move out of the hotel and into it until we have time to search for a more permanent apartment. With Alyssa moving in with Dexter, her apartment still has time left on her lease. If my season ends early, I'll have time to work with Avie to find a place. If not, she can move into the apartment which is much better than a hotel room," Jermony explained.

"Well, I guess that's something. It's a good thing Jermony found you, huh?" Kimberly said to Avalon.

Jermony stood to end the discussion when he saw how abrasive Kimberly was trying to be, on purpose.

"Avalon, until you are on your feet, we're family and I got you. Kim, come help me make sure everything is in my bag," Jermony said, taking her by the hand and walking out of the room.

Avalon quickly put her shoes on, grabbed her bag and car keys and left the house. She didn't need to stick around to hear them fight about her. She was used to people having arguments where it concerned her and she didn't want to end up having Jermony hate her and no longer wanting her around because his wife already hates her. She was used to being in the world alone.

Just as she reached the brand-new Honda Accord that Jermony bought for her, Avalon felt her cell phone vibrating in her purse. Searching the Coach bag for it, she sighed unhappily when she saw who the text was from; it was her mother. Ginny was the one person she hoped would turn into someone different than who she was. Their interactions were never good and even now, her fingers shook nervously as she checked the message. The few words on the screen frightened her. They read, *"you still owe me and I'm collecting."*

Avalon threw the phone in her bag and jumped in her car. She sat in silence for a moment before banging her fists hard on the steering wheel, scaring herself when she hit the car horn by mistake. She started the car up quickly before Jermony or anyone else came out to see what was going on. She didn't want anyone to see the tears that began falling from her eyes. She realized her own mother was never going to allow her to escape her past.

3

DJ stood at the head of the conference room table and looked around at his team of security officers who were gathered for their daily meeting before the start of the next shift. The full team was divided into three, eight-hour shifts and he made it a point to work with each team several times throughout the week. He, himself worked twelve-hour days and sometimes longer depending on the crowd and any special events that occurred like concerts or major fundraisers, the latter of which he was about to bring up to be sure they all knew what to expect.

"Okay, guys, lets settle down. There is a little over an hour before your shift starts and as usual, thanks for coming in early so that we can go over a few things. One of my security managers, Clarence, who is new was going to be working with you today, but I needed to move him to a later shift because it's Friday night and we're expecting a huge crowd for the fight that's occurring here at the casino, our first professional boxing event. Some of you who will be working the early shift today will get a few hours in the middle of the day to get some time off before reporting back tonight. I'll be here throughout each shift, so if you need me, each of you know how to reach me or any of the five managers because we're all on duty tonight."

"Because of the fight, we're expecting lots of celebrities, right?" Lawrence, one of the members of the security team asked.

"Yes, but don't lose your job by being a fan tonight. Do your job. That's your main priority, not trying to snap photos, selfies or get autographs. Stay on task. They come here and expect top-notch security and that's what I expect you to give them. A lot of them will have their own security and we've requested information on who'll be bringing extra security so that we're aware. When I say security wise, things will be tight, it will be like you've never seen before. The arena here seats seven thousand and the fight is sold out. There is a big VIP event after the fight and a lot of you have already been told you will be on hand for that. You should have all received your individual assignments and also who you'll be partnering with when you do your rounds. I expect vigilance in the parking garage for those of you stationed there and identification will be scanned for anyone going in or out of the garage, even those on foot; no excuses. Their passes to the fight are linked to their government identification, so when you scan the passes, make sure the face matches. No one can sell their pass or give it to another person. Any issues, the holding area is ready and waiting for any problem attendees," he said.

DJ was about to continue when Torrence and three members of his leadership team entered the room and stood to the back. After everyone acknowledged Torrence, DJ offered him a few minutes to speak if he wanted to. He had been told that Torrence was coming into the meeting for each shift, but he didn't know if he planned to say anything.

DJ signaled for him to take the floor.

"No, I'm good," Torrence replied. "I'm just here to observe and not speak."

DJ nodded and went back to his meeting.

"Okay, so fellas, let's take a look at the screens around the room which show traffic that's currently on the three gaming floors. Now, I know guarding the restrooms is a thankless job, but we want women to feel safe and secure coming to our casino alone. No one has to stand in the hallway at all times, but make sure during your rounds, you pass by that area. Of course, cameras are always on in the hallway leading that way, but there is nothing like having actual eyes on every aspect of our gaming floors. Because of the large number of celebrities expected, there will be extra security on all floors including the suites and condominiums. There is extra cleaning staff on for tonight and remember to always check their identification throughout the night with random checks. They know that at any time, they can be asked to produce identification that will be checked and rechecked. Safety is always the number one priority. We have several new people we've added to our list of those to watch for and you'll see those faces and names appear on the screens on your left. Their information will be sent to your phones before your shift. Be diligent about keeping your eyes on their activity. We haven't seen any of them yet, but we've received information on them from other casinos that have experienced some issues including two brothers who tried to literally run out of the casino with chips they swiped from a table. Things will be crazy and wild, but stay alert. These three screens are showing the main floor and on first glance, what do you see?" DJ asked Sebastian, another member of his team.

"Damn! I see a woman so fine, I'm already distracted from even knowing my own name! Who is that? I promise to invite all of you to our wedding!" he shouted and the room broke out in laughter.

DJ looked at the screen and to his shock, he was looking at Avalon in a body hugging little black dress that formed to every one of her sexy curves. Her long hair flowed down her back and with her usual confident and determined walk, she was drawing the attention of not only the men in the room with him, but from every man and woman she walked past on the floor. With elegance and grace, she sat down at one of the blackjack tables and glanced around. He felt it odd the way she was looking around as if she was expecting someone to walk up any minute. He'd seen her at the casino four of the past seven days, but he didn't venture in her direction, deciding to keep his distance from her, though he wanted nothing more than to go to her for answers that he still wanted and needed. Clearing his throat, he brought the attention back to the meeting.

"There are a lot of beautiful women that come into the casino and I expect you to not let even one of them deter you from what you're on the floor doing. While you were gawking at her, you didn't see the guy at the next table swipe chips from the person sitting next to him at the gaming table? Did anyone catch that?" DJ asked.

He smiled when Torrence raised his hand, as he expected the boss would do. Torrence was all business when he was at the casino and he knew not even the love his life,

Reese, could take his eyes from business of the casino floor.

As he looked around, DJ noticed no one else had raised their hand.

"That's what I'm talking about. Those guys were a plant for this exercise. I know you're not on shift yet and you all are good at what you do, but even now, while we're going over what's coming up, I need you to stay focused," he exclaimed.

"We got you, boss, but you have to admit, she is the most beautiful woman any of us has ever seen. Look at her. I've seen her in here all the time for the past two weeks or so. She always comes alone, but she doesn't always leave alone and, how could she? Look at her," Sebastian said.

DJ looked to Torrence who smiled at him. Only he and Torrence knew about Avalon and he was planning to keep it that way.

"Focus guys. Let's look to the screen to the right and see if anything is out of place there. I'm going to step out for a second and let Byron take over. He'll be another manager on site during your shift."

DJ walked out of the conference room and into his office across the hall followed by Torrence. Sitting behind his desk, he looked up and waited for what he knew was coming next; a conversation about Avalon.

"I know we haven't talked much, but you know I'm going to ask about what is going on with you and Avalon and is there anything about her that I should be concerned about. Jermony told me about her problems in New York and I know you were seeing her back then and how that all went down. Jermony is a good friend and a powerful friend. A few days ago, he asked me to consider her for an office position here at the casino. He said she wanted a job on the floor, but neither of us thought that was a good idea. He's trying to keep her out of trouble and figured a place like the casino with all this security around would be a good place for her to start to redeem herself, but if you think even having her in the administrative wing will be too much and risky, let me know now," Torrence said.

DJ rubbed his early full beard which reminded him he needed to get a shape-up before his next shift. He was thankful there was a top of the game barbershop in the casino. He was tossed between telling Torrence to not trust Avalon and also figuring a job in the administrative wing would keep her off of the floor and out of the way of temptation. What he couldn't answer for, and he hoped it wasn't noticeable, was his maddening desire for her. What was wrong with him? The woman was hell on heels!

He let go of his inward struggle and thinking that she could perhaps be looking to turn her life around, he didn't want to stand in the way of that, though he knew he needed to keep his own distance from her.

"A job in administration will be fine. Maxine, your office manager, will keep her in line and just like with the casino, there are cameras everywhere. I don't think there is anything to worry about, but as you know, she was involved with some pretty heavy hitters in New York and they are now unemployed. She wasn't the ringleader in all that went down, but she played a role in distracting men and getting them to do things that they wouldn't usually do," he said.

"Is that what she did to you?" Torrence asked.

DJ shuffled in his seat, hating the fact that what Torrence just said is exactly what happened to him. He was blinded by her beauty and her way with men and he got caught up. He didn't expect a woman so beautiful to be so toxic.

"I fell for her hard. I've told you that. Even now, I still think back to what actually happened and I honestly don't know how I missed so much of what was going on," DJ said. He was still pissed off at himself.

"Jermony told me that she had a life coming up that shocked even him. He wasn't making any excuses for her, but just because she's beautiful, it doesn't mean she didn't have a hard life. According to him, she has pretty much been on her own since she was a teenager, making due the best way she could and she found that her looks got her in doors she never thought she'd get into. In other words, she used what she had to get the things she wanted and needed and connecting with powerful men who gave her whatever she wanted became her way of survival. Have you really talked to her since you saw her, what a week or two ago here at the casino that first time?" Torrence asked.

"No, just briefly that night. Before then, I hadn't talked to her since the night we were both taken in for questioning by the FBI."

"Wait. Nothing? Do you know what happened from her perspective? I assume you would want answers. Listen, one thing I know about moving on is that you'll need answers or you're never free of what happened. She got out of that situation unscathed and here you are, though doing great now, you see her and I see the tension it causes. I can tell you still have feelings for her. I saw your reaction when Sebastian ogled her through the screen. I saw your quick show of anger at how he and all the other men were looking at her and then you quickly wiped it away with a phony smile," Torrence said.

"I do and I can't shake it. Does that make me crazy?" DJ asked. He was happy he could freely talk with Torrence. Once Reese connected the two of them together, he had the utmost respect for Torrence who flew all the way to New York to be the confidant, brother and friend he needed. Since their first meeting, he shared things with Torrence he'd never shared with anyone else.

"It doesn't make you crazy. It means you have a heart even if she stepped all over it. Remember, I told you about me and your sister. Back in college when we first hooked up, I was head-over-heels in love with her and she treated me like crap. She cheated on me and though I was all in with her, she wouldn't give me that kind of commitment, but still, I was all about her. Even after I caught her with another guy back in my sophomore or junior year, I still loved her. Sometimes we can't control where our heart lies. Thankfully, I reconnected with her later in life, though that wasn't the ideal situation either because then I hurt her by seeing other women. It wasn't until I told her everything, that we were able to start the healing process. I didn't know if we would get back together, but I was able to give her the answers she needed to why. I think you need that. She's here in Chicago, so talk to her. If you find that you still care about her and your heart is with her, then don't let what happened stop you from going where your heart wants to go. We all make mistakes and that includes Avalon," Torrence explained.

DJ had a question on the tip of his tongue and he was hesitant to ask it because it could mean a risk to the casino. Torrence would understand his reservation.

"What if she's here with another scam in mind? What if there is a scam that could involve the casino? I'm one of three guys who are head of security around here and as much as I keep telling the guys to watch for distractions, Avalon could still be a distraction for me. I saw her on that screen and I felt the same way Sebastian was bold enough to speak about. She's not only beautiful, which is what they see, but there is more to her than that; good and bad. She's a fiery combination that excites me and terrorizes me, especially if she's still on her game," DJ admitted.

"Well, then, the only way to find out is to talk to her and stay close. You're an officer and you've learned from the past what to look for. You expected to know and see too much so early in your career. It's okay to make a mistake and you were completely cleared from that New York scandal. The moment you told me you had nothing to do with what went down, I believed you and do you know why?" Torrence asked.

"Why?"

"Because I know you and I trust your character. You would never get yourself roped into doing something illegal, not even for a woman as beautiful as Avalon is. Man, back in college, your sister was the male version of what I had turned into after college. I remembered all of that and the moment I saw her again here in Chicago, I wasted no time trying to get back with her even though I knew my stuff was messy with a woman in Vegas and that wild chick in Dubai. I wasn't sure Reese was good for me, but she was good to me and that's all I remembered. Today, I love her more than anything and I can't wait to make her my wife and start popping out little babies with her. Our issues were not as bad as what you and

Avalon went through, but it doesn't have to be. Figure it out so that you can keep your mind on work and make sure Avalon isn't here trying to work us. I respect her brother and he's a good friend, but unlike New York, if she's up to something, she's not getting off the hook. I want to add her to a list of people to watch out for, especially of those she encounters. She may have a new scheme in mind, but we'll be vigilant and you'll do your job first, that much I'm sure of. If you want, I can get someone else to keep a close eye on her. I thought maybe, you'd like to do it," Torrence offered.

DJ leaned back in his chair and swiped his hand across his face in total frustration. Torrence was right on many levels. He did want answers from Avalon and if she needed to be watched, he had to be the one to do it. She would be suspicious of anyone else. They had history and he knew her better than anyone else involved in the casino.

"You're right and I can do it," he said.

"I know I was right when I put all my chips on betting on Black. You've got this covered. We have a lot riding on tonight, so get back to your men and make sure they're ready. We'll be swamped with check-ins soon and I want the lobby security team triple staffed. We have extra front desk help coming in and the restaurants are double staffed tonight as well. This fight is huge for us. We've had big events before, but this is the biggest. I want to talk to you more in-depth next week about the fundraiser for City Council President Tucker Glass who is running for Mayor. He's announcing that Carter Garrison will serve as his campaign chairperson," Torrence admitted.

"What! Really? Carter? That's awesome and a great honor," DJ acknowledged.

"It is and Reese is stoked since she and Sienna are best friends. He's even hiring your sister's marketing firm to lead the marketing and promotion campaign for the election. He and Carter have been friends a long time and they serve on some of the same boards around town. I want to go all out for this fundraiser, which will be a casino and concert night. More when we talk. For now, let's get ready for tonight and show our guests what we're all about! We want people gambling, drinking and having a good time," Torrence shouted.

DJ stood and shook his hand as Torrence left the office. Before going back to his men, DJ went around his desk and turned on all of the security screens around his office. There were forty cameras in all that he had view of from his office with most being on the gaming tables. His eyes again landed on Avalon and if he was going to find out what happened in New York and if she was up to something now that she was in Chicago, he would have to confront her and there was no better time than the present.

4

As soon as the dealer put down Avalon's last card, she shouted with joy when she noticed her cards totaled twenty-one. She loved the excitement over knowing that all she had to do was wait to see if the dealer bottomed out and the minute he placed a king on top of his sixteen, she knew she'd won. It wasn't a gigantic win because she hadn't bet a whole lot of money, not spending all of the money Jermony had given her, but it was a win in her column. She danced in her seat as the dealer counted out her winning chips. She was trying to decide if she should play a few more hands or move on to something else. She was passing the time until the big fight later that night where Jermony was able to get her a ticket. It wasn't a front row seat like she had hoped, but at least she would be in the arena and could lay eyes on some big-time celebrities, a huge benefit of being Jermony's half-sister. If she could just get DJ to see her on one of the million cameras she knew were throughout the casino and perhaps come say hello, maybe she could get the chance to explain and apologize, something she hadn't been able to do in New York. She been whisked away so fast that by the time she saw him again, they were being taken into separate interrogation rooms. That was the moment when she realized how much she had come to care about him.

Even while she was under the spotlight, all she cared about was making sure that the FBI understood that DJ had nothing to do with what happened. She had used him without him knowing about it because she knew if he had known, he never would have stood by and let anything illegal occur. She was happy when eventually, Jermony told her that DJ had been released, though he was no longer a New York City policeman. She thought he would fight it, but he didn't and she blamed herself.

"Miss, are you playing?" the dealer asked.

"Oh, I'm sorry, yes, I am," she replied.

"No, she isn't. Don't count her in," DJ said.

Avalon turned around at the sound of his deep, baritone voice, the same voice that gave her chills when he whispered in her ear at times when their bodies were flush against each other – times she missed every night when she went to bed alone. She missed his touch, his caress and most of all falling asleep in his arms feeling safe and loved.

"Hi," she said turning her seat all the way around and taking her chips from the table.

When her eyes locked with his piercing, black pools of heat, her body's temperature rose to meet the heated glare. Her mind went to New York and the number of times she looked into those eyes and fell harder and deeper in love. Not hard enough to back away from the plans that were already in place, but hard enough that she missed him like crazy. After coming to the casino day after day hoping to see him, she finally got her wish.

"Avalon, right?" DJ asked.

Avalon took that snide question because she deserved it.

"You can call me, Avie. It's what my friends call me," she said, stepping down from her seat and standing before his full six-foot four height. She loved how he towered over her. She loved tall men.

"Then I won't call you that because we're not friends. I'm just checking to see if right now you're Avalon or Justice. I'm not sure who you are these days or what persona you're taking on. Perhaps there's a new name I don't know about that you're using in Chicago," he said.

Avalon let out a sad sigh. She wanted nothing more than to have a chance to really apologize for the embarrassment he went through because of her. The way he looked at her said all she needed to know right now and that was that he hated her while her heart and he body still yearned for him.

"I deserve that," she said.

"I hope you don't think that's all you deserve," DJ whispered.

When he leaned down and spoke close to her ear, Avalon felt her body tremble with the heat of his breath close to her neck.

"You want to do this right here? Right now? I could get into all of this with you right now, but I'm not sure you want to do that. I'm assuming there are eyes watching everything that happens on the floor. Do you want to answer for what anyone is seeing right now? If they're looking hard enough, they may see my nipples are hard because I'm not wearing a bra, just some pasties holding this big puppies up," Avalon said looking up to where a camera could possibly be and knowing she was also getting a rise out of him. "You know what whispering to me does to my body. Unless you want everyone to see, I don't recommend any more whispering close to me," she added and smiled up at him while she faked fanning herself.

"This is not the time or place for flirting. I've been under your spell before, so I know what it looks like. I'm not trying to do anything right now. I'm just wondering why you're here in Chicago and what's the angle. Is it the casino? You've got something going on here that I should be worried about? Did you know I worked here before you got here? Did you think it would be easy to run a scam around me again? If so, don't bet your panties on that," he said. "I'm not the same DJ or Black that you knew in New York," he added.

As DJ leaned in close to her ear for the last part of his sentence, her body shivered again when he said the word panties and her legs quivered on top of her stilettos. She loved how he enjoyed sliding her slinky underwear down her legs and the way his fingers would softly caress their way down her legs.

She was turned on, but she was also hurt. DJ's questions came out with such force that Avalon could sense the hurt and pain behind each word. Each one cut her like a knife puncturing her skin.

"I'm not running anything and I'm here because my brother invited me here. I didn't know you worked here. I admit, I remember you telling me you were from here, but I had no idea you were working here. I do admit that once I knew that, I've been coming back in hopes of seeing you. I wanted to talk," she said.

"Talk? About what?"

"Well, you must have wanted to talk to me too. I know

you've seen me here over the past few days, but today, you approached me. You didn't do it just so that I would know you were here. I know when you're near."

Avalon leaned up to say those words. If they were going to play the whispering game, she wanted in on a little bit of that. Back in New York, they loved whispering close to each other's ears to see who would give in first and begin their passion-filled, heated exchange that would lead to some of the best sex of her life. She found enjoyment in sex, but not like she did with DJ. With him, her need for his touch became obsessive. The man had skills that would ravage a woman and have her practically begging for more.

When DJ moved back from her, she sighed unhappily. He abhorred her and she never wanted that. His reaction to her was stiff and rigid and not in a good way.

"What?" he asked.

"I know when you're near me. I can feel your presence. I know you hate me, but we had a connection and hate didn't dismantle that," she said.

"I don't hate you. Hate isn't part of my character. I am hurt that you clearly kept things from me and you lived under a name and didn't think enough of me to be real with me. I was real with you and more open with you than I had been with any female. You trampled on that and still, I didn't get any explanation."

"You were gone," she said.

"What?" DJ asked.

"You were gone. I tried calling you after everything happened and your number was disconnected. I didn't know how to reach to you to explain and say that I was sorry."

"I'm listening," DJ said.

Avalon tried to form her words and looked around at where they were standing in the middle of the gambling floor. This was not the time or the place. She wasn't sure he would be open to a more private setting to talk. He probably picked a private place to protect himself, not physically, but emotionally.

"Can we get together and talk privately? I mean, at a place that you feel comfortable being alone with me. I know how things can be between us when we are alone and I wouldn't want any old vulnerabilities to resurface," she said.

"Oh, really. You wouldn't? Are you trying to play me right now? I know you're good at that and all, but again, I'm not falling for anything again and I don't have a problem being in any place with you. I already know nothing is going to happen," DJ said harshly.

Avalon felt that distance growing with every word. Looking into his eyes, they told a different story, but now wasn't the time to play on that. She also remembered the text from her mother and she knew that she had to pay up and being in a casino, she was surrounded by opportunity to pay her mother off, hopefully for the last time. The fact that DJ ran security could be used to her advantage, but she needed a way to make something happen without dragging him down again. She couldn't forgive herself if his life was turned upside down again because of her. She knew he was going to try and work her to see if she was planning something and this time, she had to play it close to her heart. Too much went wrong in New York and this time, she was operating on her own. She'd learned a lot from the streets, but was she ready to run game on a major casino?

"Can we have dinner over the weekend or next week? I

know you're busy with the big fight tonight and other festivities here this weekend."

"You're going to the fight?" he asked.

"Yes. My brother got me a ticket before he flew out to his game."

"Look at that. You're living the high-life and you didn't have to rip anyone off to get it; or are you? Is Jermony really your brother or is that some kind of game you're spinning?" DJ asked.

Avalon was about to respond, but instead, her disappointment at what DJ thought of her got the best of her. She turned and briskly walked away. Turning her head to the side, she could see DJ following her. She stopped when she saw a hallway to her left with no one in it. She turned around and quickly came face to face with him where he practically walked into her.

"Listen, I admit, I was wrong for what I did in New York. I was in deep and I couldn't get out. There are things you don't know about that I can't explain away in a few minutes here, but don't insult me about running game on family. Jermony found me; it wasn't the other way around. I did a blood test before I even knew who he was. Yes, he's my brother. We have the same father. Yes, he's been doing nice things for me since he found me and I have unselfishly accepted his help, but I'm not running anything on him. Right now, he's the only real family I have. I don't have anyone else in this world right now, but him and I'm trying to take a better path in life with his help. I don't expect you to understand because you've always had family and you didn't have to worry about how you were going to eat or where you would live. I have and until you walk in my shoes, don't judge me. I want to explain and apologize for misleading you and if you'll give me the chance, then do that, but don't keep bringing up snide comments about my character and what I've done. I know what I've done. I lived it and I'm trying to do better," she said through gritted teeth, to keep from crying.

Avalon huffed so hard, she could hear her heart beating rapidly in her chest. She watched the show of emotions playing out on DJ's face and wondered if he would turn and walk away this time. When he didn't move, she waited.

"I can't do dinner and I don't think that we should. We can do lunch, but not here at the casino. I know a place, but only if you are going to come with answers and not try to talk your way out of what happened. I'm angry and hurt and definitely disappointed, not just in you, but in myself for letting you get one over on me, but not again."

Avalon placed her hand on DJ's arm and removed it quickly when he looked down at where her hand was as if it were a snake about to bite him. She then realized, she needed to tread lightly. She needed to stop acting as if they are picking up where they were before they turned onto the street back in New York where the gala was and the FBI appeared out of nowhere.

"Sorry. I didn't mean to touch you since you look like you are about to jump out of your skin. Lunch at a place you choose is fine. When?" he asked.

"I'm not off until Monday," he said.

"Oh, I can't Monday. I have an interview with the casino for an office desk job. I don't know how long that's going to run," she answered.

"I'm off Tuesday during the day. I have to be at the

casino at midnight that day. Does that work?" he asked.

"Yes, Tuesday. What's the address to the place where you want to meet?" Avalon asked. "I have a new cell phone if you want the number so that you can text it to me or if you know it just give it to me and I'll add it to my notes on my phone," she said.

Again, she saw all kinds of struggling thoughts running across DJs face, which she knew had to do with him questioning exchanging numbers again. She decided to let him take the lead and she'll hang back, unlike what she is use to doing.

"What's your number?" he asked.

Avalon read it off to him as he put it in his phone.

"Text it whenever and I'll meet you there. I guess I'll see you around sometime this evening," she said.

"I guess you will since you seem to like hanging around the casino a lot. Are you going to the VIP event after? Did Jermony get you a ticket to that?" he asked.

"No. I'm just going to the fight and then back to my hotel."

"You're not staying here? I felt sure you would have gotten a room since the fight could run pretty late and you would be out on the road really late at night," DJ said.

"No. I like where Jermony has me for now. His wife didn't want me at the house, though he never said that, but I got that vibe from her," she said. "I may be moving into Alyssa old apartment or my own place soon depending on when Jermony is off the road with games. Kimberly may have an impact on that too, but it's a waiting game," she said.

"I guess you're rubbing all kinds of people the wrong way, huh?" DJ asked.

When Avalon saw the regret on his face, she decided to not strike back with her own hurt over his comment, especially when it was true with Kimberly. She was another woman who didn't want her around, just like her own mother.

"I'll give you that. He put me in a nice place. After he comes back from the road, whether they are in the final game or not, we're going to look for a small apartment for me, especially if I get the job. I know you don't believe it and that's fine, but I'm really trying. Sometimes the past won't let go of who you're trying to be, but I'm trying hard. I guess I better let you get back to work," she said.

"I'm not on yet. I saw you on the security monitor while I was talking with my team," he admitted.

"And you couldn't resist me?" Avalon asked and smiled. She was disappointed when he didn't smile back at her, but at least she'd made a little progress. They were having lunch in a few days. She had enough time to figure out what she was going to say in hopes that she wouldn't drive him further away. They had issues between them, but she missed him more than she was willing to admit. She wanted to be held by his arms. She wanted to have a comfortable, uninterrupted night of sleep knowing he held her close and wouldn't let anything happen to her. He was the first person to make her feel like she wasn't alone in the world and in one night, that was all snatched from her.

"I'll see you Tuesday," DJ said and walked away.

Avalon watched him leave and that stride that was all DJ wooed her. She watched his long, purposeful and full of power legs head off onto the casino floor and she kept her eyes on him. She had experienced her share of men and though she still felt young at twenty-six after her recent birthday, she'd lived the life of a thirty or thirty-five-year-old woman. Men came and went, but DJ was the only one who left a lasting impression. His touch was electric. She felt like every burden in the world was lifted when he held her tight in his strong, muscular arms. She loved running her fingers through his full, soft beard and times when he made sweet love to her, she would hold onto his head and let her fingers run through his soft, short cut hair. She loved playing with that one diamond ring in his ear and when she kissed it and sucked it into her mouth, she would drive him mad with want. She wanted that again. DJ may be trying his best to fight his attraction to her, but she knew men and she knew him. His words were fighting words, but his eyes were lovemaking eyes.

When her cell phone vibrated, she grabbed it thinking he had sent her the text with the address of the place they were meeting. She was excited about having his number. When she saw her mother calling, she grimaced and answered.

"Not now Ginny. I don't have any information for you. I'm trying," she said.

"Try harder or you know what's coming. You wouldn't want your famous brother to have to explain who his half-sister really is and what kinds of things she's done in her young life. He won't want you around if he finds out and I would hate to have to blow up his perfect life with tales for the media of the sister he now holds dear to him. I need money and a lot of it. You messed up in New York. That was supposed to be a huge pay day for me with what your cut would have been. I know you're in Chicago now and your brother has millions. I'm sure he wouldn't mind parting with some of it to keep me quiet, so you better work it out. You said you were hanging at some new casino. Maybe you can talk some sweet older gentlemen out of their chips or you know, use those womanly ways you are known to use to get what you want. Isn't that how you tempted one of my boyfriends, years ago? I know you blame me for everything but you were a little minx back then and you used yourself. It wasn't just me," Ginny sneered through the phone.

Avalon paced nervously. She hated when her mother brought up the past as if that was something she needed or wanted to be reminded of.

"I said I would get you the money and I will. It's not easy after what happened in New York. There are eyes on me, especially from my brother and he isn't going to just cough over a hundred thousand dollars to me. I'm going to try and work the casino end and see what I can do. I just found out I have a brother and I don't want to ruin that by scamming him out of money. I can't do that!" she yelled.

"You can and you will or you'll regret it. Send me some pocket money. I'm running low. I bet he's giving you playing around money. Send me that. You can always get more. I need it by Sunday. I have rent to pay and I'm already three months behind. They are threatening to evict me and Reggie. A couple of thousand will do. If you can't get it from him, I know you have other money stashed away. I'll be at Western Union on Sunday at noon, the usual spot. Money better be there waiting for me," Ginny shouted into the phone.

Before she could get another word in, her mother had disconnected the call. Avalon was left staring into space trying to understand a mother who would blackmail her own child with her past. The things she had done that even now still disgusts her, were things her own mother had put in place to benefit herself. Ginny was still taking from her and she had a feeling she always would. For now, she would get her the money she wanted. She did have some money stashed away for a rainy day from other scams she'd run in the past. She was again between a rock and a hard place with no way out other than to use tactics she learned from the streets.

As she walked toward the ladies room with her shoulders slumped, Avalon knew she was again a lost cause. She would either have to get money from Jermony which was hard because she would have to tell him the truth about her past and she knew he would never look at her the same if she did or she would have to figure out a casino angle that could once again put her on the hotseat with DJ. Either way, someone was going to get hurt and she would end up on the run again and living in a world alone. She was tired of losing. She was tired of owing for her past sins, things that occurred before she was an adult. They were also things that could ruin her life and maybe the image Jermony had for himself and his family if he was tied to her.

Finding an empty stall at the end of the row in the ladies room, Avalon went inside, grabbed a bunch of tissue and held it up to her mouth as she cried, so that no one would hear her. Too many of her days ended up this way and she was tired.

5

DJ jumped when the weight of Reese plopping down on the sofa next to him shifted under her weight. When she hugged him tight, he smiled, considering how tense he was at the start of their family dinner, he was feeling pretty good at the end of it.

"I'm glad you finally came to dinner to meet David. He's not so bad, huh?" Reese asked.

Pulling her tighter, DJ placed his arm around her shoulders while he flipped from one cable channel to the other while relaxing in the family room of Reese's new place. She and Torrence had begun building a new house some months back and now that it was finally finished, he was glad to get his first look at it while also spending an evening grilling his mother's boyfriend, who by the end of dinner, had won him over. He had reservations for no reason.

"He's not bad at all. You understand why I felt some kind of way about him, right? I mean, our father was not only a terrible father, but he was horrible to our mother. She was a doormat for him and I saw things first hand. I couldn't understand how she could still want him all those years even after he left us and started a whole new family. She hasn't had the best of luck with men," DJ said.

"Well, her luck wasn't all our father's fault. Mom had her own issues that made life hard for herself. She has a mean streak and having David in her life seemed to calm that streak. She and I have come a long way from the ups and downs of our relationship. You've always been her favorite as the only boy and she's missed you so much while you were in New York. We know you left because of our father, but I'm glad you're back. Mom is happy now and I love the change in her. You see how much David cares for her?" Reese noted.

"Yeah, he really does and I'm happy for her. Dinner was great by the way. Where is everyone?" DJ asked.

"Mom and David are cutting us all slices of pie and Nicki, once again, slipped off to take some call or something. Have you seen how different she is? She seems so strait-laced and focused, not that it's a bad thing. She was so unsettled about what she wanted to do with her life and now she has plans and smiling and giggling into her phone. There must be someone new in her life and she's keeping her from us," Reese shared.

"Her? Is she sure of her sexuality? At one point, I know she was working through something and not quite sure. That's how I learned the definition of fluid."

Reese giggled.

"I know. Me too. She explained it very well and I told her that no matter what, I would be here if she needed me or just needed to talk as she worked through understanding her life's choices. I know she went out with a guy a few weeks back and she said she had a great time. Whoever this is, and I think there is someone, this person must really mean something to her. I don't like that she's keeping whoever it is from us. She's our baby sister and I worry about her."

DJ was worried too, but he knew Nichelle could handle her own love life. He had enough problems with his own life to not have enough time to get all vested in someone else's.

"Well, secret or not, let her have her space. She's entitled to work it out and will come to you if she needs advice. She always does, so don't worry. I only hope this person is as into her as she appears to be into them. There is nothing worse than putting your heart on the line only to have a knife stuck through it and all the blood drained out of it," DJ lamented.

"Oh, wow! That chick did a number on you. That was a brutal image you just shared and I don't like it. One woman doesn't control your heart, especially if she didn't handle it well," Reese explained.

DJ turned around to face her while they waited to be called back into the kitchen for pie.

"You and Torrence went through a really rough patch and I remember how much he hurt you, but you still loved him. I mean, I know you fought it and held a straight face through it all, but you shared with me that though he crushed your heart, you never stopped loving him, even when he was begging you to give him another chance and you wouldn't. What made you forgive him? He did you wrong and even if he owned up to it, that had to be a big pill to swallow. What finally drew you back to him because the two of you are just sickening in love with each other? I've never, ever seen you this happy and you don't do commitment. With Torrence, you only have eyes for him and he's the same. How did you get over the hurt?" he asked.

DJ smiled when Reese patted his hand before

explaining.

"Torrence hurt me so bad. I told you that he was the first guy I ever told that I was in love with him and he was actually the first guy I ever wanted to say it to. We had a rough time back in college, but I contributed that to being immature and I wasn't ready for the feelings I was developing for him. I played it off by seeing lots of guys and having fun, which is what the college years are for. Fast forward to present day, or over a year ago, we reconnected and I thought that the time was right. He was doing all the right things, saying all the right things and things just seemed so perfect. I saw the love between Carter and Sienna and you know what they went through and I thought they were as perfect of a couple as perfect could get. When she divorced him for cheating on her, I thought that love had died as far as I was concerned. I figured if they couldn't make it after being in love from our first year of college, then all hope was lost. When they got back together because Carter fought hard to win her heart back, I regained my faith in love again and I realized I wanted that. I was tired of casually dating and having men in my life who thought texting instead of talking was leading to some kind of a relationship. Torrence was different. He wanted to talk and he didn't care what time of day or night it was. We would text little things and he would send me a sweet text every day and he put his all into what I thought was us falling in love and I was all in," she explained.

"And then the bottom fell out, right?" DJ asked.

"Oh, it sure did. This woman showed up out of nowhere and I find that he had been screwing her and another woman in Las Vegas when he went there where his other casino is.

For the first time in my life, I put my all into someone and that's what I got; a man I loved who cheated on me. I tried to act like I didn't love him anymore, but that wasn't true. Through the hurt, I still loved him. Through the pain of him possibly going back to the woman in Dubai, I found it hard to sleep through a night peacefully. I was a mess because I was pissed off at him, but I loved him at the same time. The last thing I wanted was for him to fall out of love with me and fall in love with someone else. That would have been harder than knowing he was unfaithful to me," she explained.

DJ nodded that he understood.

"You forgave him," he uttered.

"I did and I would do it a million times. We all make mistakes and he did. I know you're thinking about what happened with you and Avalon and she made a mistake. It was a big one, a major one, but she made a mistake. The bottom line is, and I'm only speaking from what I believe and not what you've said, but I think you're in love with her and you're too embarrassed at what she did to you to admit it. I almost lost Torrence for good because I kept pushing him away because of the hurt. I think everything can be forgiven. I looked at Sienna and Carter and how she was able to forgive his transgression. He vowed he would never let her go and he didn't. Not even after she divorced him. You know about me and Torrence, but also, did you know what happened to Dexter? He had to forgive Alyssa for not telling him about the baby she was carrying that was his. He didn't find out until she was about to deliver. They struggled to find equal ground to live on, but they did just that in the end. We can all overcome everything. Look at mommy," Reese said.

"She's forgiven our father, hasn't she?" he asked.

"She has. She hasn't forgotten, but she forgave him so that she could move on with her life. You can live on hatred and unforgiveness. Mommy is so in love that she and David introduced Torrence's mother to a man that she's in love with and thinking about moving in with. I know you remembered that drama between mommy and Torrence's mother. It's about finding that love that works for you, not what works for everyone else. This is about you. Do you have deeper feelings for Avalon than you have let on?" Reese asked.

Without trying to hesitate, DJ knew he needed to be honest.

"I do and the moment I saw her in Chicago, I realized even after what she did, my feelings haven't changed for her. She entered my life and was vibrant, sexy, loving and fun to be with, while at the same time, she could talk about politics as easy as those her age talk about social media. There is a five-year age difference, but it didn't seem that way. I fell hard for her and I was lost when I was pulled into her drama. She really did a number on me and every time I see her, I want to scream and holler at her while also wanting to pull her into my arms and kiss her until I feel the need to breathe. I really thought she cared about me. We had gotten really close, or at least I thought we had. I don't know now. I think it was all a part of her game plan."

DJ forcefully leaned back on the plush sofa, exhaling out of frustration at himself for still having feelings for a woman who was a scam.

"But you see her and you can't stop thinking about her. Do you think you could ever forgive her? Is there any future for the two of you? I ask because I think back to when you told me you were thinking of proposing to that other woman and then things tanked because you found out you weren't ready. Not only were you not ready to be married to her, but you realized she wasn't the one for you at all and you ended things. You survived that. When you told me about Avalon, who was going by Justice then, I could hear your excitement through the phone. I've never heard that much happiness from you before. Avalon has her issues; we all do, though hers are a little out there," Reese laughed.

"Yeah, they are. I admit I do miss her and the way she keeps flirting with me, she misses me too. I don't want her to just forget about what she did as if it wasn't major. We can't go back to the moment before we were taken into custody," he explained.

"Then don't. You don't have to go back, but you can move forward. I'm not telling you to jump back into anything with her, but if you need to lay it all out with her, then do that and figure it out. If she's for you, you will know. I think a part of you knows that she needs a man like you and it's possible she doesn't know how to trust anyone like that. I don't know a lot about her, but Sienna said Carter shared that she had a rough upbringing and that's all she knew."

"I got that part. I don't know the depth, but I think it was pretty bad. She's never talked about it other than to say she doesn't have any family that she can count on. When I asked about her mother, she would tense up. I could tell that was a bad subject for her. I now know that she and Jermony have the same father and I do know the story with him. That's been in the news before when people dive into Jermony's background. You can't be that high-profile without someone trying to dig into your life. I'm having lunch with her in two days," he said out of the blue, hoping to get it out there, hitting Reese with the shock factor so that they can move on from the conversation about Avalon. From the stunned look on her face, he didn't achieve his goal.

"What? When did that happen?" Reese inquired.

"I saw her at the casino the night of the fight on Friday and she wanted to talk and explain what happened back in New York. I guess I still need that closure, so I agreed to meet her. I'm second-guessing it now though. She's trouble, no matter how you look at it," he admitted.

"Do you think she's not being sincere?"

"I don't know. I think she may be up to something. It's hard to tell. I couldn't tell before and look what happened. She's in Chicago now and could be working at the casino soon," he said.

Reese sighed and DJ knew why. Torrence must have told her about the interview.

"Yeah, I heard. At least it's not on any of the gaming floors. In the administrative wing, which is not even on the casino grounds, she'll be out of trouble. Not much to get into there," Reese reasoned.

"True, but that doesn't mean she won't find a way. She's a master at playing men and I'm not just speaking about me. That twenty-five-year-old was involved in something major that got the chief of police, the chief of detectives, my captain, the mayor and the commissioner all placed on the unemployment line and she came out like pure gold. She wasn't in it alone and I know that. There were tiers of people who she got involved with that even involved some madam who was getting women for all those men I just mentioned, who are or were all married at the time. This thing was major and yet, here she is breezing through life like nothing happened. How can I trust anything she says?" DJ asked.

"You trust your heart. You watch your back and take more care in what her true motive is. If she's still up to no good, I think now that you've experienced her, you know what to look out for."

He knew Reese was also looking out for Torrence and the casino.

"I won't let her hurt Torrence or the casino. She will never get over on me again, I can tell that as a fact. She hasn't seen this new version of Black 2.0," he joked.

"Black 2.0? Oh, tell me more about him!" Reese laughed out loud.

"Pie!"

They turned toward the kitchen when their mother screamed.

"We can table that chat for another time. You always help me see clearer when we talk and I appreciate it," DJ said.

"Are you still going to meet her on Tuesday?" Reese asked.

DJ stood and helped Reese stand.

"I am. I admit I still care about her and I miss her, but I also need to know what she's up to without her knowing I'm keeping an eye on her. I'll keep her close," he said.

"Baby brother, you better watch yourself keeping her close. You could get caught up again and lose your focus. She's young, but she's apparently smart."

"Tell me something I don't know. Tuesday it is. I hope to get answers and maybe those answers will give me insight into why she's really in Chicago. I know she's enjoying getting to know Jermony and his family, but I don't think that's it. I think there's more to it," he said.

"Black is on the case though, right?" Reese asked.

"I'm on it. Fool me once, shame on you, fool me twice, yeah, I'm not going to let that happen!" he exclaimed and followed Reese into the kitchen.

6

"I like this apartment. It's the perfect size just for me," Avalon said as she followed Jermony and the leasing agent around the small, one bedroom, one and a half bath apartment which came with a full living room, dining room and even a small sunroom. There was a nice, big kitchen, though she didn't cook much. She got excited over the white and gray décor and she loved the stainless steel appliances in the kitchen. The walls were white, crisp and clean and the dark brown hardwood floors gave the place the aura that spoke of money. Thanks to her rich brother, she felt like she now had money too, something she didn't have to beg, borrow or steal to get; a first for her.

"You're close to work now that you got the job at the casino and you're only thirty minutes or so from me. I think this location is a good one," Jermony said.

Avalon nodded as her head continue to turn left and right to check the place out. She wanted to do a little dance in place, but she decided against it, thinking she would look like a woman who never had anything.

"True. Thanks for getting me that interview earlier today

with Torrence. For the most part, I interviewed with the two office managers and they liked me. Torrence told me that he didn't tell them about my past because he wanted to give me an honest start, which I appreciated," Avalon explained.

What she really wanted to say was that no one had ever given her the benefit of starting over before. She'd been thanking Jermony since the moment she found out they were related, but he told her to stop because it's what he should be doing to help her get back on her feet. She kept to herself the fact that he had no idea what she'd been through and how much she needed someone to actually be in her corner without wanting something from her.

"Yeah, he told me about that when I spoke with him when I landed today."

"So, the season is over for you, huh?" Avalon asked.

"Yeah, we lost the game, so we're out, but that's fine. There will be next season and I get to spend more time with my family. Kimberly brings the kids to the home games, but I would prefer that she not fly them all over the place for away games. She provides the stability at home that our kids need," he said.

"Yeah, something I never, ever had. There was nothing stable about my life."

Avalon looked up as Jermony turned to the leasing agent.

"We'll take this one. Can you draw up the lease and I'll co-sign it? We'll be down to your office in a few minutes," he said.

Once the agent was gone, Avalon walked over to the large sliding glass door that led to a small balcony attached to her fifth-floor apartment.

"I've never had anything of my own as far as a place to live. I've always stayed with people or had roommates where we barely made rent and a few times I've been evicted because of having no money. I hope I'm not taking advantage of you being my brother. I appreciate all that you do, but I know this can't be as easy as it seems. I know how complicated I am – something you don't know the half of yet. There's a lot about me that you don't know. I'm not a really nice person. I have a past and I understand why your wife doesn't like me. Women can sense things in other women," she said.

Avalon tried to muster up a smile as Jermony came close. Since she first arrived in Chicago, his wife has been pretty clear that her presence isn't welcomed in their lives. It's not even about her not being open to new family members that Jermony may find, but she knew it was a vibe considering the kind of life they live and the life she has led, living from place to place and the biggest issue, the way she has scammed people. She knew Jermony shared that with his wife, as he should have, and because it's all true, she could fault Kimberly for her feelings. She wanted Jermony to like her not just as his sister, but as a person. She had doubts about her own ability to do and be better.

"Listen, I can't speak for Kimberly. You'll have to build that relationship with her yourself. I can't make her like you. You have to earn that. I'm your brother, so you don't have to earn that with me. We're blood and that's all I need. I've waited a long time to find you and our other brothers and sisters and I'm not turning my back on you," Jermony said.

"You'll be the first person who doesn't. It's been pretty rough out here for me. I'm not trying to have a pity party, but that's just the truth. That storybook like that a lot of people life is foreign for me. I make do with what I have," she explained.

"Avie, any time you want to talk about that, you let me know. If you want me to help you find a professional to talk to, I can do that too. We've all done things and so whatever you've done, let it go. It can't be too bad now because we are going to work together to help you get your footing."

Avalon decided not to share anymore. The more she thought about her past, the more embarrassed she became. Instead, she replaced what she knew was a sorrowful look on her face with a smile.

"How is the search going for our brothers and sisters?" she asked, changing the subject as they stood together looking out over the Chicago skyline. She was glad the apartment was on the fifth floor and on a hill. She could see much of the city below.

"Finding the others isn't as easy because people only remember your mother and of course, my mother because he was married to her. As for the others, I don't think he was involved with those women here in Chicago. Our father drove a truck for a living, though my mother and I barely saw any fruits of that labor. He drove from state to state and so the women could have been anywhere. The only thing I'm told is that he would brag about all the kids he had in several area code, but wasn't taking care of none of them. He would boast about planting his seed and having all the fun without the responsibility. They are all out there somewhere and I intend to find as many as I can. We're a family and I know I need all of you and I hope you all need me too," he said.

Avalon felt bad. She didn't want him to be the person

they all needed when it came to him having money. She knew she needed it, but in her heart, she wanted having a big brother more than anything.

"I need a big brother," she said quietly. "I need family, something I've never had. My mother wasn't your typical mother. She was and still is self-serving and she was like that my entire life. Things were really bad with her and all I knew were the streets and how to get things from people to survive. I don't want to do that with you. I know you have it, but I don't want you to think that's all I want from you," she admitted.

Avalon leaned over when she felt Jermony pull her against his side. She felt like a tiny, little girl because he was well over six-feet tall. She loved looking up to him. She'd never felt so protected.

"Kid, I will always be your family and I won't let anyone hurt you or use you ever again. I hope New York was a lesson for you and that you know you don't have to do things like that anymore. Yes, I have a lot of money, but life isn't always about money. Before you say it, I know the old saying is that people with money can say that, which is true, but I mean it. When I say I need you and my siblings in my life, it's not to throw material things at you, but if I can make your life easier to help you get and have the kind of life you want, I will. Our father did us all wrong and if it wasn't for basketball in college and the help of the father of one of my best friends in the world, I may not be where I am. Everybody needs somebody," he said.

"Who is this man and who is your best friend? Is he a team mate of yours?" she asked.

"No. His name is Carter Garrison. You've met him. He

was at the casino the first time you went there. You may not remember him because I introduced you to so many people. I've never had a better friend than him. He's turned out to be more of a brother than a friend," Jermony offered.

"Wow, the way you talk about you makes him sound like a hero," she said.

"To me, he was and still is. In college, he shared his father with me and a few other guys who needed father figures in our lives. His father took us under his wing like we were his sons. He gave me guidance, he came to my games, he cheered me on and when I needed someone to talk to, he was there and I'll never forget what he and Carter did for me. I remember when I won a medal in basketball at school and I went to Carter's home during spring break one year. His parents had his medals and certificates and things like that all around their house, showing how proud of him they were. I was angry that I didn't have parents who would prominently display my accomplishments like that. Before I left to go back to school, Carter's father asked me for the medal, which I kept in my bag. I didn't know why he wanted it. He then took it, walked to the room where Carter's medals were and on one wall, they had made a huge area of blank space and that's where he hung my medal. He told me if I ever wanted to have a place to display them, that he'd just created one for me. Since then, if you go to their house, I have just as many medals in their house as I do in my own house," Jermony shared.

Avalon didn't know how to react. She'd never met people like Carter's parents who had so much love that they shared it outside of their family.

"Carter didn't mind sharing the spotlight since he was an

only child?" she asked.

"Not one time. In fact, when I would win something, Carter would remind me to drop it by the house and add it to my wall of fame. He is my lifelong brother. They became the family I needed when I thought I had no one. I was on scholarship and it didn't cover everything. I would work like crazy, but Carter's father saw something else in me. He wanted me to focus on school work, so each semester, when I got my scholarship money, he supplemented what I needed to cover food, books and other essentials to the point that I didn't have to work when I finally started playing ball. He told me I had a future playing ball and he was right. To this day, I could never, ever repay him for the strong presence he was in my life. I tried to buy him things, but he wouldn't hear of it. He's well off himself, but still, I felt like I needed to do something for him. He told me to just continue to make him proud and that was enough. For me, it wasn't enough, so I did gift him with front row, floor seats to every Chicago game. When I play home games, he and Carter are always right on the floor cheering me on."

Avalon looked at Jermony with amazement. She'd never heard of a man who wasn't family but did so much for someone else.

"That's wonderful to have someone like that in Carter and his family," she said.

"I'm trying to be that for you. I'm paying it forward, not just because I have it, but because I should and I want to because that's what family does. Now, we need to talk about furniture because you can't sleep on the floor," Jermony said, looking around.

"I don't need much other than a bed," she said.

"Nonsense. You're a twenty-five-year-old woman who I know likes nice things. I've seen the clothes you wear and the bags and shoes you have. I won't ask where you got that expensive stuff you brought with you from New York, but they're all nice. I'll talk to my accountant and get you some funds to shop with. I would say don't go overboard, but make this place nice for yourself. I'm not trying to buy your love as your brother, but I am doing what a brother should do to help his sister, so let me. What else is on your plate for this week? You said you don't start work until next week?" Jermony asked.

Avalon was happy she got the job, but she was hoping to be closer to where the actual action was happening. She wanted to do right, but her mother was pressing her and rather than try to swindle her brother, she needed to work the casino angle and to do that, she needed to be at the casino to scope out the day to day activity. For now, she would do the right thing and work the job while planning out how to work those in the casino, either the lonely looking game table players or perhaps a few of the workers. She's already seen quite a few of them checking her out and flirting from a distance and she knew she could work that.

"Um, not much. I'm doing lunch with DJ tomorrow and before you huff and puff, I know you want him to stay away from me, but I told you what happened in New York was not his fault. He's not to blame; I am and he has every right to be angry. It was a crazy time and I ruined his career even though I think he wasn't happy doing it. It was still his livelihood and I did him wrong. His anger that night at the casino was warranted and you shouldn't lash out at him about it. I know it doesn't seem like it, but we were something special to each other back then, even in the midst of the scheme. I still like him," she explained.

"I got that, but why do you need to have lunch with him? What does he want? I don't want him berating you. That could lead to tension between me and my friends, especially Torrence and Reese. What's really going on?"

Avalon shifted nervously from one foot to the other trying to explain without angering him.

"I asked for a meeting with him. He came up to me in the casino Friday, the night of the boxing match. We talked a little and he was still so angry. We were involved for almost six months and it was pretty intense. We really cared about each other, but I didn't know how to be involved with someone like him. All my life, people have taken from me and had expectations that satisfied them, but never me. It wasn't until after everything went down that I realized DJ was nothing like that. I mean, I knew it before hand, but I was in too deep with the scheme. He really cared about me. It wasn't just physical – it was much more and I didn't focus on that because I never had that before, so I didn't know how to live in that. My life wasn't filled with people who cared about me like I now know he did. My schemes weren't just about me, my mother pushed me into them too and it was hard to understand where my loyalties should be. I should have chosen DJ," she explained.

"Because of your mother? Why didn't you tell me any of that when I first found you? That was about four months before everything happened. I offered to bring you to Chicago then and you didn't want to come. I had no idea you were running scams to benefit your mother and yourself of course, but for your mother to ask you to do illegal things, I will never understand that. What mother does that? You don't have to worry about that anymore. You're out of that game and here in Chicago with me and my family. There is all love here for you. Let's go down to the leasing office and get the paperwork signed so that you can move in. I know you need a bed, so get that first and whatever else you want, work that out. For what it's worth, I'm glad you're here. I wouldn't want things any other way," Jermony said.

Avalon exhaled and held tight to Jermony when he pulled her into a tight hug. She'd never felt anything like the instant feeling of love she received from him. He truly cared about her and the feeling of being loved unconditionally was something she'd never experienced; until DJ. She held many regrets about their time together. She was getting a new opportunity at life and she still felt like any minute, someone would jump out and tell her that her recent luck was all a fluke and she still had no one. For now, she was still trying to take it all in. She felt loved when she was involved with DJ and now, she knew what she felt for him was real love. He didn't ask her for anything, he didn't ask her to do things that benefited him – he tried to show her what a *real* relationship could be like and she threw it all away. She couldn't lose another man; she couldn't lose her brother. She had to figure out a way to get her mother out of her hair without revealing to Jermony who she really is.

"Let me take one last look around as I'm thinking of things in my head. I'll meet you there in a minute. I want to look around the bedroom one last time. Okay?" she asked.

"Don't take forever. I know how women can be when it comes to their minds being on decorating," he joked.

Avalon shooed him away as she walked back to what

would soon be her bedroom. As she entered as her heels clicked across the brown hardwood flooring, she walked to the center and danced around like a crazy woman. She wasn't crazy – she was excited! She'd never had her own place without there being strings attached or others she had to share space with. This apartment would be hers and hers alone. If she could just get away from the past that keeps coming back to haunt her, she would be okay.

New York was a test and she skated through. Her mother was trying to turn Chicago into her life in New York and she couldn't have that. There was too much at stake and it wasn't just Jermony, but it was DJ. She really hoped they could start over and find that good part of them together as a couple, but only if he would accept her apology and believe that she would never hurt him again, at least not on purpose.

As she left the bedroom, she walked by the large bathroom with a shower separate from the tub. She'd never seen anything like that until the suite at the hotel where she was currently living and of course, the house the Jermony lived in. She'd never seen really nice things until Chicago. She had things in New York and even money, but she had to make all that stretch to cover her for rainy days, and she'd had many of those. Her life was looking better now and she was hoping rainy days were in her past where she wanted her past life to be. She turned and looked at herself in the floor to ceiling mirror on the bathroom wall between the sink and the tub.

"You're on the move now girl and there's no stopping all that you can be from this point on," she said to herself. Her mood changed quickly when her phone rang and the North Carolina area code showed up. She struggled with answering, but knew that if she didn't Ginny would keep calling.

"You have horrible timing, Ginny. I sent you your money and I know you picked it up. I don't have any more money right now. I sent you all I had," she exclaimed.

"Child, I'm not calling about that money, at least not at the moment. I'm calling to see if you've asked your rich brother for what I *really* want. I know you don't have it, but he does. If not, I was thinking of using the money you sent and getting me a train ticket to Chicago to meet him myself. Besides, I'm practically family since the same seed that made him was all up in me too at one time or you wouldn't be here. Work on that other money, that big pay day for me, child and I'll call you back in a few days. I need that money. I went to the library and looked him up. I saw on the internet that he is living large and I know you're working him to get what you want. That's all you know how to do. Figure it out and get me that money and no more of that nickeling and diming that you've been doing. I'm talking big, big money! I would hate to have to show everyone who you really are, so make it happen!"

Again, before she got the chance to say anything in response to her mother's curt words, Ginny disconnected the line. Out of frustration, she was about to slam her phone into the sink and then came to her senses. She wouldn't break her phone because her mother was a horrible person. Every time she felt like she was taking a step or two forward, her mother was dragging her back down to the gutter. What was she going to do other than get the money so that she could get on with her life? There had to be a way. She couldn't live with herself if her brother or even DJ knew about her past. None of them would love her after finding out.

7

With the alarm clock blaring like his apartment was blowing up, DJ reached across his bed to the nightstand to turn it off as his head pounded from exhaustion. He'd spent an extra shift at the casino and had to push his lunch with Avalon to dinner because he was so tired. When she replied back to his text that dinner would be fine at the same spot, he came home and laid across his bed without even taking off his clothes. Other than his shoes, he was still in his all black suit and tie, a staple outfit for him. As he sighed, still feeling the results of two busy shifts, he thought back to how he got his nickname, Black.

As a kid, he had been pushed around a lot and the bullies came for him on the regular. He didn't have the best clothes as his mother struggled to make ends meet on her own while raising three kids. One day after getting another beat down for his lunch money, he walked home and encountered an older teenager who told him that he was tired of seeing him walking home beat up and bruised. That was the day his whole life changed. The guy, whose name was Buster, told him that being bullied was a mindset, something he allowed.

He had to learn to stand up to bullies and not be pushed around and for him, it was all about the look. DJ found out that he wasn't the guy of boy a guy would shy away from and that he had to change his look. Buster told him to get new clothes. When he said he couldn't afford them, he told him to put on whatever he had that was black from his hat to his tennis shoes. If he couldn't afford them, get a black marker and color his shoes and hat black. He knew he had black pants and a black t-shirt at home. Buster told him how to walk and how to have swagger. The next day, he went to school in his all black with a confidence that he didn't have before. When the same bully approached him, he didn't back down. Instead, he let his all black with swagger do the talking for him and it worked. When he walked home from school and saw Buster later that next day, he thanked him for showing him how to be a little more confident and claim his space. After that day, people rarely saw him without having all black on and everyone started calling him Black. The name stayed with him and he liked it. He even loved DJ, but he hated being called by his given name, Delvin. He was a junior and he hated being reminded of the man he was named after.

Rolling over on the bed, he thought about texting Avalon and cancelling for the night. He had to be back at the casino early the next morning and he was already exhausted. His days and nights lately had been long and to say his free time wasn't spent doing anything constructive would be an understatement. These days, he spent his free time wondering what Avalon was doing and what she was planning. Seeing her again brought back old feelings that he wanted to leave in New York along with all the drama, but he couldn't escape her. Every time he looked on a screen at the casino or checked out tapes from shifts when he wasn't there, he saw her and each time, she was even more beautiful than the last. When he had time to get home and get some sleep before heading back to work, his dreams were filled with nights of them together. At first, it was about the great sex and then their time together turned into so much more. He had even loved the way she softly snored and even now with his night alone, he longed for that sound to break up the silence. His body remembered everything about her too and he was hoping a night of talking over dinner wasn't his greatest regret of being unable to resist her. He never could before.

Hopping out of bed to make it to dinner on time, he grabbed his cell when it vibrated on the night stand. He came to life when he saw a New York phone exchange. It was Diego.

"Diego! What's up brother!" DJ exclaimed.

"Nothing, except for the fact that it's taken me seven or eight calls to you for you to finally answer my call. You left New York and just left it all behind. What's up with that? I thought our friendship was better than that. You had to know I would be concerned about you and my wife is trying to disown you for the way you've treated us, ignoring my calls and messages. You good?" Diego asked.

"Yeah, man. I'm good and apologize to your lovely lady for me. Things have been crazy here in Chicago since I came back. I did tell you that I got a job at the new casino here, right?" he asked.

"Yeah, you did. It's owned by your sister's fiancé, right? Is that the one?"

"Yeah, that's it and the job is going well. I'm one of three guys who head up security force for the hotel. The hours can be maddening, but it's worth it. I love every minute of it."

"So, you're recovering well after what happened here? Man, let me tell you about things here. Everything is so different and there is all new leadership in place at all levels from the lieutenants all the way to the top. They really cleaned house after what your girl did, no disrespect by calling her that. I know it wasn't just her, but she's the only one of that crew that I knew. I hear there were like fifteen outside people and of course all the guys on the force. Your girl Justice was small fry compared to the others involved," Diego shared.

"Avalon," DJ interjected.

"What? What's Avalon."

"That's her name. Her name wasn't Justice. That was a personal she made up. Her real name is Avalon and guess where she's at right now," DJ offered.

"Jail, I'm assuming, though everything was done under cloak and dagger. All we know is people were reassigned, fired or they quit. I'm assuming the perpetrators of the scheme are all behind bars by now."

"Not all of them," DJ said walking around, pulling out clothes he was going to wear, of course in all black.

"What do you mean by that?"

"Avalon didn't go to jail and she's here in Chicago," he said.

"What? First, you're saying her real name is Avalon and also that she's in Chicago with you? That's crazy, especially after all that mess she was involved with and how it cost you your job too!"

"I know, I know, but she's not here with me. It's a long story, but trust me, she's not with me. She has people here and those same people got her off the hook. After all that went down, she walked away without a scratch on her or even a hint of anything on her record. It pays well to know people, I guess," DJ said.

He didn't mean to talk down about Avalon and her brother, but that was how he felt. There were no repercussions for her and he didn't understand that. He was hoping to learn more over dinner.

"I just knew she was the one for you. I would see the two of you together and there was no doubt about the chemistry between the two of you. In the time that I've known you, I've never seen you look at a woman the way you looked at her."

"That's because I never have."

"Are you seeing her still, now that she's in Chicago?" Diego asked.

"Not really. I mean I've seen her, but not seeing, seeing her. I'm meeting her to talk tonight, but that's it."

"You sure? I know how you were with her and I don't see the two of you just talking."

"Things have changed."

"Be careful dude."

"I am. How is everything else in New York? What am I missing?" DJ asked.

He often thought of going back for a visit, but he knew all eyes would be on him. There were plenty whispered once he was let go from the force and the timing was right when everything happened. The only reason Diego knew as much as he did about Avalon was because of their close friendship. The night of the gala event was going to be the night that people would finally see him and Avalon together and then word would be around that he had a woman. He preferred keeping his private life private and he now knew why keeping things private didn't bother her. She didn't want anyone to know who didn't already know.

"Are you finally wearing anything other than all black?" Diego jested.

"Funny. Of course not. It's not that I never wear other colors other than black. I just prefer Black and now with the new job, I can afford even more black. I promise you, my closet has colors other than Black and I switched up a time or two when I was in New York. You just never saw it."

"Lies!" Diego shouted and DJ laughed out loud. "I hope you're planning to visit New York when you have time. Not everyone is a fan of what happened to you and even if you don't believe it, you have lots of friends here, starting with me. I miss my partner."

"I know you were scrutinized since we were partners and I apologize for that," DJ lamented.

"Yeah, but it was cool. The only reason you're not here is because of your connection to Justice – I mean Avalon, otherwise you would still be on the force. You were a casualty that had to happen, but we all know that didn't make you guilty of anything."

"That's because I wasn't. That didn't mean I don't feel guilty about what happened, but it's water under the bridge. I can't keep living under that spotlight. Life goes on," DJ said.

"True. Does it go on with Avalon or is that done?"

DJ waited before he answered. The truth was things weren't completely over until he gets the answers he needs and he was getting that tonight.

"It will be done by the end of the night. I can't go back," DJ admitted.

"Nothing says you have to. There is always a new future. Keep in touch, man. I may come your way and check out that new casino. The wife and I were talking about taking some time away and we may make that time away in Chicago to check up on you. I'll let you know if we do that."

"Do that. It will be good to see you both."

After ending his call, DJ checked the time and knew he needed to get moving to meet Avalon.

Turning on the shower, he stood at the sink in the bathroom and thought back to the last time they were together in New York before they were picked up.

The night before, she had come to his place, unexpectedly. He didn't think he'd see her knowing that she had several beauty appointments scheduled to prepare for the gala event. He had worked the night shift, getting off at midnight and was surprised to find her sitting on the steps of his brownstone when he got home shortly after midnight. The one thing he loved and hated was that she had no fear. Avalon could walk the streets of New York and scare of the biggest and most determined criminal just with a look. She was bold and he could tell she had survived due to her street smarts. He respected that and sometimes her fearlessness scared him. He worried about her all the time.

After explaining to him that she'd had a full day and was going crazy not seeing him until the gala. She had tried going to sleep in her apartment, but her roommates were making a lot of noise and she wanted some peace and quiet, but only with him.

They went inside his place, where they fed each other fruit on his sofa before she announced she was going to take a shower. Needing to go over a report he was working on, he told her he'd meet her in the bedroom when she was done. Minutes after hearing the shower run and then shut off, he turned to see her standing in the doorway of his living room in nothing but a pair of high-heeled red pumps and nothing else other than a pair of handcuffs swinging from her fingers. Her body was everything and she knew it with confidence. She moved her hips as she sashayed over to him. Her nails were painted in hot red and her lips were covered in a bright red gloss. She was all about business and he was ready to be her client. His tongue was glued to the roof of his mouth and words escaped him. He'd never seen a more beautiful sight. When he did try to speak, she had silenced him with her finger, running it back and forth across his lips.

He looked to where she still held the handcuffs and she made it clear that they were for her wrists, not his and his body convulsed with the thought of having his way with her.

When she kissed him, her lips told a story without using words. She quickly helped him remove his clothes, which they did in record time with his eyes focusing on every movement the handcuffs made. When he was naked, he picked her up and took her to the bedroom. While he reached for the condoms he knew they would need throughout the night, he turned around to find her lying flat on his bed with her legs open and her arms stretched toward the corner bedposts. When she asked him what his plans were for the cuffs, he proceeded to show her and where he thought he was going to be in control of their love making, even with her handcuffed to his bed, she was in control. She moved her body around in ways to had him feeling like he would die from being so turned on. She knew how to gyrate her hips in just the right direction to give him the most satisfaction. With her hands cuffed, she used her legs to clasp them tight around his hips when he entered her and the things she did with the muscles within her womanhood had him howling again and again. He was thoroughly exhausted by the time the morning came. By then, he was waking up to his arm being in the cuffs and he smiled, giving her the okay to secure his other hand. As soon as she did, she didn't use anything but her mouth to bring him to the brink of passing out from her tantalizing caresses. He was done for and she knew she had him in her grasp. Their sex life was off the charts, but deeper than that was his love for her. Why did she have to mess it all up? Why couldn't she come to him if she needed help?

Realizing the shower would soon be running cold water, he hopped in and got through his shower as quickly as he could. He had a dinner date to get to and some questions to finally have answered.

8

Checking the time once again, DJ thought that perhaps, Avalon wasn't going to show. She was almost an hour late and he was growing impatient. He was just about to call her when he looked up and she was walking toward him like something out of one of his dreams, the one's he'd been having about her lately. The air in the room collapsed around her and for an instant, there was no sound to be heard. His focus was on her and only her and her beauty. He didn't think it would be possible for her to get any more beautiful, but he was wrong because she was.

Walking toward him, she was in short, flowing denim skirt, with a white shirt tied at her waist with a denim shirt underneath. On her feet were her usual high-heels, also in denim, no doubt some kind of designer brand. She carried a small denim Louis Vitton purse. Her hair was down around he shoulders in her usual natural twists. His eyes darted immediately to her gorgeous lips and his desire to taste them had him shaking his head frantically to get rid of the immediate ping of need he felt whenever he was around her. Tonight, it was particularly strong. She was smiling bright as if they weren't about to talk about a more dismal time in their lives. That was typical her and he knew it. No matter how bad things were or could be, she was always smiling through it.

"Sorry, I kept you waiting," Avalon said as he stood to pull out her chair.

"I was just about to call you," DJ said.

"You were worried?" she asked.

"I was, but that's my nature to worry when it comes to women. It's a man's job to be protective," he explained.

"Even of me?"

"Yes, even of you," DJ answered as he sat.

"I see this is a night of all black. As you always do, you look dapper," Avalon exclaimed.

"Thanks. You are beautiful as usual, but this isn't a typical date night of compliments and I don't want to stray from our reason for being here," DJ warned.

"I know. Can I order a drink before you grill me?" she asked just as their waitress walked over.

DJ nodded his head toward the waitress and waited while Avalon ordered her signature Sangria while he ordered another soda. Alcohol was something he never drank. He preferred strong sodas and coffee when he needed it. After the waitress left, he tried to make small talk before jumping into what he really wanted to talk about.

"I heard you got the job. Congratulations," he said.

"Thanks. I'm excited about proving myself and I appreciate Torrence giving me a chance. I also got an apartment yesterday. Jermony signed for it, but I intend to may my own rent payments now that I have a job. He paid for the first few months until I have some money in the bank from the job. I've never had my own place before. I've never had a brother before either," she said.

DJ noticed a hint of something sad in her voice. Usually nothing got to her, but there was something different about her as she spoke about Jermony.

"How did things come about? You never told me about him. I found out after you were in custody and it turns out he worked to get you out. When did you find out he was your brother?" he asked.

Before she could answer, the waitress was back with their drinks and asking about appetizers or if they were ready to order.

He watched as Avalon looked up and smiled.

"Can I have a few more minutes? I haven't looked at the menu," she said.

"Absolutely. I'll come back in a few minutes to check," the waitress said before she walked away.

"What's good here? You said you loved this place," Avalon said.

"I like salads, which you know, so they're a hit with me and so are any of the fish dishes. I'm having a salad with salmon and grilled shrimp. I try not to eat heavy in the evenings."

"I'll have the same thing. I love salmon and shrimp and salad works. What was your last question?" Avalon asked.

He wasn't planning to dive right in, but there was no time like right now.

"I asked about Jermony. When did you find out he was your brother?"

"About three or four months before everything went down," she answered.

"You knew about him and you didn't tell me? Why? Why keep that from me?"

"I don't know. It was new and I didn't know what to do with the information. I'd never had family that cared about me enough to look for me the way he did. I was trying to deal with it."

"Jermony has more money than anyone could throw a stick at and you were out here hustling people for yours when you didn't have to. Why didn't you stop what you were doing? What was the draw to keep it going? Was it the money or the reward of ripping people off?" he asked.

"I don't know. I swear, I really don't. It was all I ever knew. I only knew how to survive by taking. It's not a secret that I know I'm beautiful. Men have been after me since I was a little girl and I learned early that they would do anything to get close to me. I got connected with the wrong people," Avalon explained.

"How did you get caught up with men as powerful as the commissioner?"

DJ had so many questions, that he was careful to space them out. He didn't know if he would get this chance ever again. Besides, diving into the questions helped him take his mind off of how good she looked tonight. He already felt the need to shift around in his seat because of his reaction to being close to her again. What he should have done was what women do all the time to keep themselves from getting aroused and sleeping with a man simply because they were horny. He should have brought himself to an orgasm in the shower before meeting her tonight and he would have made it without thoughts of how adventurous their sex life was. He was already imagining them in his car with her straddling his lap and lifting her skirt while he moved her panties to the side; that is if she was wearing any. She was known to go without them on occasion. His body leaped to life at the thought.

"Through one of my roommates. She worked for a local madam as a high-end prostitute. I met her when I first landed in New York with no place to go. She tried to convince me to get in that life, but I wouldn't. I went with her one night to a secret party and all I had to do was be good company without any sex being on the table. Sex for her was a given, but the men also wanted girls who would just party with them and make them feel desirable. That was my job and I did it well," she said.

"Yes, you did. I should know, right?" DJ asked, facetiously. He didn't like feeling that he was still in her clutches. He hated that he ever was.

"It wasn't like that with you. I know I can't make you believe me, but I really cared for you then and I still do. I know I don't have a right to, but I do. For what it's worth, hurting you was my biggest regret. I didn't even fear going to jail as much as I feared what my secrets would do to you," Avalon tried to explain.

DJ brushed her sweetness and heartful apology away. He wanted to hear more.

"The party?" he continued.

"Oh, right. The party was given by your commissioner and I was shocked to see him there. Also, there was the mayor and a lot of other politicians and major players in the stock market. I was hearing names and taking notes to later look them up and when I did, I knew that I could use what I knew. Things grew from that moment on. Your commissioner wanted to try and buy me, but I wasn't interested. I wasn't a hooker or a good time girl. I definitely wasn't a mistress to be hidden away in some apartment somewhere to be at his beck and call. My roommates were into that pretty deep and had money flowing from a lot of those men. I knew some guys and I hooked them up with the information about who was at the party. They started blackmailing those guys and as payment, the commissioner and some of the other higher ups in the department would share information about empty houses of some very rich people in New York."

DJ put up his hand to stop her.

"Are you saying, these powerful men helped you and your friends plan robberies to keep you quiet about the extracurricular activities? That's cray and so far-fetched," he said.

"It may be, but it's true. It would have continued if we hadn't gotten caught. One of the men, not sure which one, leaked information about the bribes to the feds and that's how we all got caught up. Big robberies were planned the night of the gala and if it hadn't been for Jermony, I'd be in jail with the rest of those guys. The one saving grace is that none of them know my real name. They only know me as Justice. I learned to never use my real name while I was in the streets. It was for protection and I learned to not trust anyone," she said.

"You didn't trust me enough to share who you really were? I get it in the beginning, but eventually, I thought things were going somewhere with us. I need to ask this because it's been bothering me. When we met, was it by coincidence? Did you and your friends really have trouble with your car?" he asked.

Before Avalon even got the chance to answer, he knew what she was going to say. The way she was avoiding looking at him in the eyes were a sign that she was ashamed of the truth, but he didn't care; he needed to hear it. "Go ahead and say it. I can take it," he added.

"I knew who you were. Your captain put me on to you. They wanted to know what guys they could trust to be a part of what was going on. He set us up with a lot of guys and I hate to say it, but most took the bait, but you didn't. I could tell from that first night that you were not the kind of guy they were looking for, but then the play became to keep you close to keep track of what you may be able to find out that could hurt them. I got into it for that purpose, to watch you and to play you, but that first night when we had sex, I was blown away by how good it was and I really liked you. I'd never vibed so well with anyone like I did with you and I couldn't walk away. Moving forward to months later and all I can tell you is that my feelings for you were really. They grew over time and I went from being close to know what you knew to being close because I'd fallen for you and didn't want to lose you. I tried to find a way to tell you everything back then, but that time never came. I could never find the words. I hope you believe me when I say I'm sorry and I didn't mean to hurt you or ruin your life. You made me feel things I'd never felt before. No one ever cared about me the way you did. I was living two lives and didn't know how to stop. The street in me was fueled by the scams and I admit, I made a lot of money, some I still have in various accounts. I saw that as my survival. I was also torn because of my feelings for you," she said.

"You couldn't have had feelings for me and kept all this from me. You laid with me night after night, day after day and it was all a game to you!" DJ shouted and then pulled back his frustration when he remembered they were in a public place; his decision when she asked if they could meet and talk.

The waitress popped up just as he was about to dive in deeper. He gave her their orders and they were then left to continue the conversation, but he was at a loss for words. He had learned more than the thought was actually going on. All the people involved was crazy and it all started from a private party with hookers and mistresses. He definitely didn't know about any of that.

"I wasn't one of them. I see the look on your face, but I swear, I wasn't one of them."

"Were there other men when you were with me?" he asked.

"Never. Even if you don't believe me, I am telling the truth. There was never anyone else while I was with you or since then. I wasn't planning to sleep with you that first night. I didn't go out with you for that. The plan was to befriend you and stay close, but having sex with you wasn't part of it. I enjoyed being with you and didn't want that to end."

"How can I believe any of this, especially you trying to convince me that you had feelings for me? This is a lot," he said.

"You wanted to know and I'm telling you the truth."

"How do I know this isn't all a part of a new scam you're cooking up? I get the feeling there is more going on than you just deciding to move to Chicago when you had the chance to do it before and you didn't. Why now? Why work at the casino? Why flirt with me? I know you and you have been flirting since that first night I saw you at the casino. What are you trying to do?" DJ asked.

He realized he was putting it all out there on the line. There was no reason to hold anything back. She was working him and keeping him close before and now, it was his turn. He knew she was up to something, but for the life of him, he couldn't figure out what.

"DJ, I swear, I'm not up to anything. I don't have a reason to anymore. Jermony is helping me get on my feet and I have a job and have moved on with my life. I needed to be out of New York and my brother made that happen for me. I've changed and trust me or not, I still have feelings for you. I lay awake at night thinking about you and the way you would hold me, kiss me, make love to me and make me feel safe. We had a connection and that wasn't a lie."

DJ doubted that.

"Wasn't it though? It was all a lie," he said.

"Not all of it. What I felt and still feel for you wasn't and still isn't a lie. Can you honestly say that when you saw me, you didn't think about the fun we had? I know I was out of control and a lot went down, but in spite of that, we still have a connection. I saw it in your pants that night when you first saw me and I saw it on your face when I walked in tonight. I feel it right now. You want me to be honest, but you're not being honest. I know what New York did to you and I'm sorry, sorry, sorry, but I want to start over. I don't know where it could go, but I want to spend time with you so that you can see that I have changed. I'm not Justice anymore. Avalon is a totally different woman."

Once again, DJ's words were halted when their salads arrived. Rather than continue grilling her for information, they settled in and ate.

By the time their salads were done and they barely said any words while they ate, he had relented that Avalon was right. He still had feelings for her and he still wanted her. He'd had casual one-night-stands with a few women since returning to Chicago, but nothing made him feel as satisfied as when he was with her in New York. He never had a problem getting to completion with any woman, but with Avalon, he had always wanted more again and again. He could never seem to get enough. She was always as ready for him as he was for her. They were magical in bed together.

"Are you going to tell me how you ended up in New York?" he asked.

"Can I not tonight? I've answered so many questions and my brain hurts. I know tonight was about you getting answers, but I'm all talked out. Can I ask you how you've been? Something a little lighter in conversation?" she asked.

"How I've been?" he countered.

"Yes. No more grilling for now. I think you got the gist of what happened. My life before New York is hard to talk about and I'm not ready. I do want to hear about you if you want to share. I understand if you don't. I know you only came to talk about New York and you're probably ready to leave, huh?" Avalon asked and looked down at the table.

She was hurting. DJ could see it in her expression. She really didn't mean to hurt him, but she was still holding something back and he couldn't figure out what it could be. Could any of the power players from New York still have a hold on her? Was she into something new with any of them?

If he were going to find out, he needed to calm down and play her game with her. He was betting on himself for the win this time.

"I'm fine. Working like crazy and enjoying being back in Chicago around family," he said, drawing her eyes back up to his.

"Are you seeing anyone special?" she asked.

He couldn't admit he was still pining for her and so he kept that to himself.

"I date here and there, but nothing serious," he admitted.

"You mean you have friends with benefits," she laughed.

For the first time tonight, he smiled.

"Something like that," he said.

"DJ, I know all about your needs and you don't go too long without having them satisfied. I understand what that's like."

Now he was curious. Was she alluding to the same kind of relationships after they broke up? If so, he didn't want to hear anything about it. He was still soft in the heart when it came to her, an admission he wouldn't dare put out on the table.

"What about you? Seeing anyone here in Chicago?" he asked.

"No and before you beat around the bush without actually asking, I have not been with any other man since you. I haven't wanted to. I can't stop thinking about you. Do you think you could ever trust me as one of your friends with benefits?" she asked.

Bold and blunt. That's how he remembered he being and he could see that she hasn't changed in that area. She never left a person wondering what she was thinking.

"Why, Avalon? Why would you want to be that? You deserve more than to be a bed-buddy."

"True, but I don't have a desire to be anything with anyone and then you pop up and I have that need, but only for you."

When she leaned over, he leaned across the table.

"Do you know how many nights I've had to touch myself just to get to sleep? I've only done that for myself when I'm alone and for you on many occasions. I admit I need more than that, especially right now. You look so damn good in your black shirt and pants with your Gucci belt. I see that diamond in your ear still winks at me. I miss you. I know you miss me and you don't have to admit it. Your pride won't let you admit that though I am a terrible person in your eyes, you still find me attractive," she said.

"I will always find you attractive. A man would have to be blind to not see that."

"Desirable, still?" she asked.

DJ knew they were playing with fire, but he was already far beyond caring about getting burned. He's had women, but when his mind takes him to his time with her, all bets are off. He wanted temptation.

"Always desirable," he responded.

"Come home with me. No one will know but you and me. I don't have much in my place, but my bed was delivered today. Feeling adventurous?" she asked.

9

Avalon used her key to let them into her apartment which had been freshly cleaned, but not yet full of furniture. She was planning to take care of that later on in the week. For now, all she needed was a bed and the man who was entering her apartment behind her. She waited with anticipation in her car once she arrived at her apartment. DJ had to stop at the local drug store to pick up condoms that neither of them had. She was excited about being in his arms again.

"Come on inside. I told you there isn't much here, but it's home thanks to my brother."

She watched as he walked around checking out everything, especially the view. She already knew she wasn't planning to put up blinds or curtains in the living room window. She loved the view day and night.

"This place is nice. It's a new development. I remember hearing that it was finally open."

"Is your place in the city?" she asked.

"Yes. It's not far from the casino and I can get there quick if I need too. I also have a spot there for nights or days when I'm really too tired to drive home."

"I like your car. It's a new Mercedes?" she asked.

"Yeah. It belongs to the casino, but I drive it all the time. Carter owns a dealership and all of the cars the casino has were bought from him. You know who he is right?" DJ asked.

"Yes. He's best friends with my brother. He talks about Carter and his family all the time. He tells me how good they were to him when he was in college. I'm glad he had that. If I had someone like that in my corner, maybe I would have turned out different."

Avalon tried not to show that she was feeling sorry for herself, but thoughts of her mother and how her life could have been different if her mother was different plagued her because of all she has missed out on just being a regular teenager growing up. Instead, she had to become an adult to take care of herself and skip her teen years. Thankfully, she was smart enough after she dropped out of high school to take her GED exam and pass it the first time. She'd always been book smart, but her life dictated that books not be as much of a priority as surviving.

When she turned around and looked at DJ, he had that sympathetic look in his eyes that say he wanted to comfort her and make everything better for her. If he only knew the extent of the damage her mother has done to her, he would run and never come near her again.

"You're not all bad," he said.

Avalon felt like she wanted to cry. Even after all she'd done to him, he was still trying to console her. When she couldn't hold her tears in any longer, she began to cry and before she knew it, DJ was pulling her into his arms, caressing her back and telling her things would work out for her. She wanted things to work out for them together. If tonight was all she was going to get, she would make it the best night of her life with him.

When she leaned back and their eyes locked, in her mind, she was transported back to a time in New York when life was simpler between them. Her secrets were hers and he cared about Justice. She wanted those moments back.

Looking into DJ's eyes, she saw all the love she'd been missing since they've been apart. He may never have said the words to her, but she could read them in his eyes when he looked at her without looking away.

When his head moved down closer to hers, she was anxious for the magnetism that would hit her when their lips touched.

"Damn, you are so beautiful," DJ said.

Avalon felt his hands as they moved from her back to tangle in her long tresses. She remembered how he loved letting his fingers get wrapped up in her hair especially when they kissed and he wanted to hold her close.

Thankfully, he didn't make her wait too long. With their eyes locked onto each other with neither wanting to look away, she moaned when his lips came down softly and possessively onto hers. It was more than she remembered as he held her close and slowly made love to her mouth. She felt the heat of his minty breath against her lips and when he nudged them apart and sought entrance into her mouth with his tongue, she gladly opened for him.

Dropping her purse to the floor, she held on to his massive arms as the kiss turned passionate and she felt like she'd never get enough of him loving her this way.

"Your taste drives me wild," DJ whispered against her lips.

"I've missed you so much," she uttered softly between kisses.

Avalon wanted to cry and scream for even more when his tongue glided across her lips, wetting them. He was holding the back of her head and guiding her lips where he wanted them to be. There was no doubt that he wanted her close. In front of her, she could feel his desire for her growing as his hardness pressed intimately against her. Moving slightly to the left and right, she wanted him to know that she could feel him.

As the kiss turned wild with a zest that could only be achieved with him, Avalon let her hand slip between them as she toyed with his member through the fabric of his pants. She loved the hard, rigid feel of him. He was long, strong and wide and she could feel him getting bigger the more she rubbed him. She wanted him to know how much she wanted him. What he didn't know was how much she dreamed of being with him just like this on so many nights.

"I've missed you too," he said.

Avalon's desire went to a level she didn't know existed. She didn't think she'd ever be in his arms again, but she was and he was loving her. She wanted to feel him – all of him. Reaching for his belt, she remembered she was an aggressive lover. She didn't wait for loving to happen. When she wanted it, she initiated it. As the buckle fell away, she opened the snap and when she started to slide the zipper down, she had to break the kiss in order to look down at her work. He was already so hard for her that she didn't want to hurt him with the zipper.

"A bed," she said.

"Bedroom?" DJ asked.

Avalon pointed with her finger and pulled his lips back down on hers. She didn't like the emptiness she felt when their lips weren't touching. In the next second, she felt herself being lifted into his strong arms as he walked them into her room. She didn't care that her place was practically empty. She only cared about getting into bed and him getting into her.

When they reached the bed, they tumbled into it in a fit of laughter when DJ tripped, not expecting the bed to be where it was. The room was in total darkness.

"I guess we needed to slow down a little bit, huh?" she laughed.

"I don't want to slow down. I want your sweetness right here and right now," he said.

"You are not alone in that," she admitted.

Where she would usually enjoy tossing around with him until she was on top, she let him have his way as he rolled over on top of her. She kicked her shoes off and as they dropped to the carpet, she tried reaching for her shirt when his hands stopped her.

"Let me. I want you, but I want to enjoy every single sexy part of you," DJ said.

Avalon let her body relax and just enjoy and there was a lot to enjoy. When she raised her arms, DJ untied the shirt at her waist and pulled it and the tshirt she had on underneath up and over her head. After tossing them somewhere in the room, she felt his hands land on her breasts as he caressed them first through the thin layer of her navy demi-cup bra. When that wasn't enough, she felt his lips kiss the tops of the globes before lowering the cups and making sure his tongue found the hard tips that he loved making love to with his mouth. As he flicked one with his tongue, he used the fingers of his other hand to roll her hard nipple through his fingers, driving her wild. Her hips moved back and forth, showing him what she desired the most. By way of the light that entered her bedroom through the slits in the blinds that were not closed all the way, Avalon marveled at the sight before her as DJ leaned up and removed first his shirt and then the belt that she had already loosened in the other room. With those gone, she heard his shoes drop to the floor and she knew the only thing left that was keeping her from seeing and feeling all of him were his pants and what she knew was probably his signature boxers underneath. She heard him unzip his pants and after he slipped them off and moved back on top of her, she did let her hand slide down from his chest, to his stomach to the hard, mushroom head of his penis that poked out in search of her over the top of his boxers. She smiled knowing that there wasn't a size big enough to contain all that manhood behind that material. When she slid his boxers down a little to get a better grip, she loved that she could barely get her hand all the way around him. Her fingers were never going to touch with how hard he was. She loved the silky soft, yet hard, sturdy feel of him. She wanted him in a place that wasn't her hand.

She expected that DJ would next remove her clothes, but he didn't. Instead, he leaned down, taking is penis out of her grip as he lifted her skirt and rather than remove it, he dipped his head under it, not even giving her a second to prepare for what was next. She felt her legs being hoisted up over his shoulders as he quickly moved her soaking wet thong to the side. What she felt next had her hips rising from the bed, out of control. That first swipe of his tongue against her womanhood was all it took to have her calling his name. She tried to be quiet, but that wasn't possible. His tongue was strong and worked her over like a drum. His instrument played against her over and over and her hips moved around in sync with his head movements. She wanted to look down and see him, but her skirt was in the way. She tried to focus on a way to get it off, but the feelings his tongue was eliciting from her body was too strong to resist. He was barely hanging on.

"Yes! Yes!" she screamed, unable to hold the delight in. In the next second, DJ had her behind gripped in his hands and he worked her like never before. If she thought she had gotten his best before, she was in for a rude awakening. She was feeling like she could fly and in the next moment, that's exactly what she was doing when her orgasm rammed into her, causing her body to convulse under his tongue lashing. Again, and again, he went at her and she rode him like a rollercoaster ride. Her screams were probably waking up her neighbors, but she didn't care. This was her welcome to the neighborhood and she didn't care who could hear them. Her body was on fire. Her mind was like scrambled eggs and any minute, if her breathing didn't slow down, she was going to pass out.

As her body began to calm, Avalon thought she needed a moment to regain her senses, but DJ didn't give her long to get it together.

He was a man moving with a purpose as he reappeared from under her skirt and quickly removed his boxers. Pulling her thong down her legs, he didn't bother to remove her skirt. Instead, he moved it further up her hips, grabbed for the condom in the pack he'd picked up and tore it open with his teeth.

"More?" he asked her excitedly.

"Hell yes!" she shouted. "I want to taste you too. You know how much I like that," she added.

"I know, baby, but right now, I'm going to explode if I don't get inside of you. We'll get to that, but for now, hold on to something because this ride is about to get bumpy!" DJ yelled.

"Wait!" she yelled and he stopped. She knew he was confused, but she wanted to change positions. If she was going to really fly off again, she knew how she wanted to do it – on her knees.

Sliding from under him, she turned over on her knees, grabbed a pillow from the top of the bed and placed it under her hips. Pulling her skirt up, she looked back at him and smiled. She knew he could see her now that their eyes had adjusted to the darkness. They could see what they needed to see.

"Damn! You are so sexy and wild and you know me so well. Hold on baby!" he said.

Avalon did just that. She gripped the edge of the bed, getting a handful of the comforter and probably the sheet to as she waited for exactly what she needed.

Her body was ready to rise to the occasion again the minute she felt his hardness at her entrance. With his hands on her hips to hold her in place, she pushed back as he surged forward and they screamed in delight together. After that, it was game time. They moved together, body against body. He pushed into her and she moved her hips back to meet his thrusts. He made her feel so full. He was filling her completely. His groans mixed with her moans and the slippery sounds of their love making didn't allow her to hold on for too long. DJ had been the first and only man to ever give her an orgasm through penetration and as the feeling rose in the apex of her thighs, it spread throughout her body. She was racing to get to her second climax and just as she was ready, she heard DJ tell her that he was there.

"With me, baby. Come on, and come for me baby! I feel your legs twitching. I feel it rising in you like it's rising in me!" he screamed and his words sent her over the edge.

Avalon let go with a howl that sounded like there was a wild animal inside of her. DJ grunted louder and louder as she felt the heat of his essence stream into the condom as wave after waved crashed over them together. She placed her face down in the pillow to try and drown out her devilish screams while her body thrashed about like a she-devil in heat. She was having an out of body experience. Her orgasm peaked again and again as if it would hold her in its grips forever. She never wanted to come down from this kind of high. She'd missed this kind of loving and couldn't believe she had risked it all back in New York.

As they floated back down to earth together, Avalon couldn't stay up on her knees any longer. She was losing the use of her legs with that orgasm that stole all of her strength. When she collapsed onto the bed, she felt DJ fall on top of her and then roll to the side. She knew that he didn't want to crush her with his weight. Neither could speak as the only sounds heard in the room were of their increased breaths. When DJ pulled her over into his arms, she went happily and wondered if this was the last time she would have him like this. She had invited him to come back to her place for this sexual encounter and they even talked about the casualness of what it would mean, but now she knew she wanted more. She wanted all of him again, but she didn't think he would take the risk of falling for her again. She was already beyond that point. She was in love with him. She had been in New York and she still was now.

What she wanted was for the night to last forever. Her body was so relaxed and she was so comfortable in his arms again that she couldn't think of any words to say because sleep came quickly.

10

DJ stumbled into work and yawned for the tenth time in the past few minutes.

"Are we keeping you awake, boss?" one of the guys on his team asked.

"Sorry about that. It's been a week of not much sleep for me," he said. What he didn't say nor was he planning to admit was that he'd had a week of sleepless nights of sex with Avalon. That first night had lasted all night long. After round one, they had both fallen asleep. He woke in what turned out to be two hours later to find that Avalon was waking him up in her favorite way. He felt her before he saw what she was doing and he wasn't going to pull away from her for anything. As her head moved up and down in front of him with her eyes locked on his, he relaxed his head back and let her get what she needed. They learned early when they met that oral sex excited them both when it came to giving and receiving.

In the beginning, she didn't know how to really please a man that way, which surprised him. He thought she was more experienced than she actually was. Over time, he taught her what he liked and she had become an expert at it. Reaching down, he moved her hair out of the way so that he could see her face as she loved him with her mouth over and over. For the rest of the night, they loved all on each other until the last of the three condoms had been used. For the rest of the week, they found reason after reason to see each other and always ended up in bed at her place. He had yet to invite her to his place, something he was planning on doing that night after he got off. The next day, was going to be her first day at work and he didn't want to keep her out too late. He was back to needing to be with her and they had fallen into a routine of spending his off time with her and today, it showed. The only thing he had strength to do this morning was to shower and shave in order to get to work on time.

"That kind of life, huh? Who's the lucky woman? She must be something because she is putting it on you. You've been walking around here grinning all week. We saw the signs even before you came in yawning today. You sure you don't need to catch a few extra winks?"

DJ chuckled. He had a job to do and being a little tired wasn't going to impact that.

"No. I'm good. I'll be in my office checking last night's tapes. Anything I need to know about?" asked the four security men who were with him in the main security room with views of the entire casino on all four walls.

"No. Last night was actually quiet. There was this weird couple in here last night roaming around, not playing but acting really strange. If I didn't know any better, I would say they were casing the place. They stood out. You'll see them on the tapes. I left a note on your desk with the time stamp of when they first appeared. They never played anything. At one point, I thought they were going to try and snatch an elderly woman's purse but a guy came up and the pair walked away. After an hour of them stalking people, we had security on them and they finally left," Sebastian said, laying out the most interesting part of the evening before. He had been off and spent it at Avalon's place where late in the evening, she started acting really strange. Her phone was blowing up and though she turned the ringer off, he could hear it vibrating. He knew that she thought he was asleep when she slipped out of the bed and took her cell phone with her. When she left the bedroom, he tiptoed out of the bed and listened at the door. He thought at one point, he heard her talking about money, like a hundred thousand dollars. She was talking soft, but he heard her say something about getting money to someone and that she would no longer owe them. He didn't know what was going on, but he was planning to find out.

When Avalon finished her call, he leaped back into the bed just as she entered the room. He acted like he was stretching and turning over. He even added a little fake snore and grunt to make her think he had been asleep the whole time.

She slipped back into bed next to him and raised his arm, placing it across her hips, after turning her phone completely off.

He woke in the morning without waking her. It was Sunday and he knew she didn't have to get up for anything, but he had to get to the casino. As he dressed, he watched her sleep and wondered what she was hiding and who was she talking to after midnight. His radar was on full alert. If she was up to something, he wouldn't be asleep on her this time; not on his watch.

"I'll check out the tape. Give me about thirty minutes and then I need a full brief on the whole night. Let me get a look at this couple and see if I recognize them," he said and left the main security office and headed two doors down to his office. Closing the door behind him, he clicked on his monitors and fast forwarded to the time stamp on Sebastian's message until the couple came into full view. He'd never seen them before, but Sebastian was right that they were clearly up to something. They had seen enough people up to no good in the casino that they could all spot them a mile away and this couple was no surprise. Who were they he wondered? From the time stamp, it looked like the woman was on her phone arguing with someone around midnight. Since there was no audio, he couldn't listen in. His interest was piqued. He would keep them on his radar.

He was about to check out the next tape when his cell phone pinged. It was a call from Avalon. Though he was having suspicions about her, he still had to play like nothing was wrong.

"Hey sweetness. Did you sleep well?" he asked.

"I slept like a log all night long. How about you?" she asked.

"I did, but I have to admit that I was bone tired this morning. You wore me out and we were asleep before eleven o'clock. I guess we've been making up for lost time, huh?" he asked.

"I hope that's a good thing. I love having you close and at my place. It looks like a real place now that I have more furniture," she said.

"Did I tell you how much I liked it?"

Avalon laughed on the other end.

"You did and I thanked you."

"Good. Listen, did you leave me in bed for a while last night? I thought I heard you talking to someone at one point or was I dreaming?" he asked.

He wasn't expecting the truth from her, but he was curious to see how much of a lie she was prepared to tell.

"Oh, I may have been talking in my sleep, but I was in bed – not talking to anyone. You must have been dreaming about me," she said and DJ almost choked on her lie. He now knew she was hiding something, but what, he didn't know.

"I'm always dreaming about you. Listen, I know we've been spending our time at your place. I was wondering if you wanted to spend some time with me at my place tonight? I know you have to work in the morning and I promise to not keep you up late and I will get you to work on time. What do you think? I was thinking we could cook some pasta together and watch Shaft for the millionth time. I can't seem to get enough of that movie," he joked.

DJ was giving her humor, but behind that humor, he was pissed. Something was going on with her and he needed to find out what it was. He hated prying, but with her track record, he was going to have to do that without her knowing about it.

"Sure, that sounds great. What time do you get off? I can meet you at your place. I have my first day of work tomorrow, but it's not until eleven in the afternoon. I have some type of orientation and new employee paperwork to fill out. You said you're off tomorrow?" she asked.

"I am. I have two meetings about an upcoming

fundraiser for Tucker Glass, a councilman who is running for mayor. He's a friend of Torrence and Carter's and Carter is being named as his campaign manager. My day doesn't start too early so that means we might be able to actually stay up late tonight," he joked.

"I'm for that if you are. What time shall I come by?"

"Let's make it around six. What are your plans for today?" he asked.

"I'm going to Jermony's house. He invited me over to hang out for the day and if I'm going to get his wife to like me, I have to be around and let her get to know me. I don't know if that's a good or bad thing," she said.

"It's a good thing. Have fun and call me later when you're leaving there. I may be able to get out of here a little earlier than usual. See you tonight, baby," DJ said and ended the call.

Now that he knew where she would be, he needed to reach out to a friend to do something underhanded for him. He knew just the person.

Reese had mentioned that Tucker Glass' head of security should be someone he should contact to have him check into Avalon if he thought something with her wasn't on the up and up. He found that something when she lied about talking to someone when he knew she had been. Checking through his phone, he found Gary's number and called him. He picked up on the first ring.

"Hey Gary. This is DJ, Reese's brother. She said I could give you a call if I needed you."

"Right. She told me you may be calling me. What do you need?" Gary asked.

"I need someone to do a little surveillance for me and it

may include bribing a leasing officer for entry into an apartment. Is that too much?" he asked.

DJ knew he was borderline asking for something to be done that was illegal, but he was left with no choice. He didn't follow up on the uncomfortable feelings he had about Avalon in New York and it had cost him plenty. If she had something going on, he needed to find out.

"Nah, that's not a stretch. I can get one of my guys on it. Text me the address let me know what you're looking for," Gary said.

"I have the address, but I can't say what I'm looking for. There isn't much to find in this apartment because the woman just moved into it. She has a history of doing some pretty seedy things, so it could be anything that would raise a radar, especially if you find anything about the casino other than stuff about a job in an office. Just tell your guy to take pictures of anything he finds and get back to me. I'll see you later today with a little something to put in his hands as a thank you," DJ said.

"No problem. I got you covered. Reese is good people and if she says her brother needs help, I'm on it. You need this done today?" Gary asked.

"Yes. Is that possible?" he asked.

"It sure is. If you can let me know when the person in the apartment is out, I can get my guy in. Leasing agents will do anything for extra money – even break the law in letting us in that apartment."

"I appreciate it. I'll text you when the coast is clear," DJ said and placed his phone on his desk.

He turned his chair to face the outside world and wondered if he was doing the right thing. He wanted to know what was going on, but then he didn't want to find out. After just one week of being back with Avalon, he had already let his feelings get in the way. He wanted her to be on the right path, but something was telling him that she wasn't and he needed to know sooner rather than later.

**

"What do you mean you're in Chicago? Why are you here!" Avalon shouted into her cell phone as she got dressed.

She got the shock of her life when she answered her mother's call just as she was trying to get out of the door and over to Jermony's house. He was expecting her to spend the day with him and his wife and kids. She'd never had a family day and she was looking forward to it, but again, here was Ginny, crushing her spirit and to find she was in Chicago was worse than she thought.

"I'm here and you need to come pick me up. Reggie and me need a place to crash. We tried staying in this bug-filled motel and it's nasty, but it's all that I could afford. I spent too much money on our train tickets. I needed to come and see what you were doing about getting me that money," Ginny said.

"I talked to you last night and you didn't say anything about being on a train," Avalon yelled as agitation set in.

"I wasn't on the train. I was in that casino you've been talking about. After a while, security was watching up when I think they got a whiff of Reggie trying to swipe this rich looking lady's purse. We left before we got into any trouble. We now don't have a place to stay, so I told him we would stay in your nice new apartment because I know you wouldn't mind. Come get us or I'll start asking people where your brother lives and I'll go there," she threatened.

"No! Don't do that. Where are you? I'll come get you."

Avalon wrote down the intersection, grabbed her keys and ran out of her apartment. She didn't know how much worse her life could get now that Ginny was in town. She never let her mother find her in New York because she had no ties there. Here in Chicago, she had her brother and with him being well-known, she knew her mother could cause quite a stink especially if she followed through with her threats. She had to find a way to get her mother the money and get her out of Chicago. Getting a large amount of money like that would be hard, but she would find a way. She remembered seeing Jermony open a safe in his bedroom to hand her money and she saw stacks and stacks of bills. If she could get in it, he wouldn't miss a hundred thousand. He probably had ten times that much in the safe. She would never be able to get that much at the casino, so she had to steal it from her brother. If he ever found out, she would lose the only real connection to family she had. What choice did she have? It was that or it was let Ginny ruin her life and possibly Jermony's too. Rationalizing things, she really had no choice. She would buy herself some time by letting her mother and her boyfriend stay at her place. She was planning to spend the night with DJ anyway. Now, she just had to keep him away from her place while her mother was in town. There was no way he could find out about her or the newness of their relationship would be over for good.

Racing to her car, she sped out of the parking lot and headed in her mother's direction. She quickly sent DJ a text to let him know that she may be a little late getting to his place because she was going to Jermony's later than she thought. She first had errands to run. When he quickly responded saying he could just come to her place instead, she had to swerve from hitting another car as she quickly answered telling him she would definitely meet him at his place later because she would be out all night. He sent her a thumbs up and then she sent a text to her brother telling him she would be late. Avalon knew she was juggling too much and that she was once again getting caught up. She could never win.

11

The casino was buzzing with the arrival of dozens of busloads of people looking to have a fun day gambling in Chicago. Since the soft opening of the casino, millions of gamers have come through the casino and DJ and his team have done their job making sure everyone played safe and as responsibly as possible. He was doing his usual check of monitors before heading down to the floor to do a walkaround. He had spent the morning frustrated with himself because he seemed to once again be getting caught up in Avalon's life and not just the good sexy part of it.

Thinking back to the night that they had dinner when his amorous desires overwhelmed him and he found himself on a mission to buy condoms while racing to get to her place. Good sense didn't set in and now, he was walking around aimlessly checking his phone every few minutes for any word from Gary's guy. He couldn't check himself to see if Avalon was still at her apartment. If he checked on her, she would probably get suspicious if he started asking all kinds of questions. Instead, he sent Gary a few pictures of Avalon and the make, model and license plate of the Honda Accord she drove. An hour later, Gary had a guy sitting on Avalon's apartment. This guy had checked for her car for blocks, but didn't see it, assuming she was probably gone. Gary assured him that the guy he selected was the best security specialist in his field and would get the job done of getting into Avalon's apartment and looking around.

The not knowing was killing him. This was why he should have stayed away from her. He had images of New York that continued to plague him all day while he waited.

Just as he was getting off of the elevator, his phone vibrated and he nervously checked it; it was Gary.

"What up?" DJ asked the minute he answered.

"Some activity. My guy was making sure she wasn't there and he saw a maintenance fella that he was able to buy entrance into this woman's apartment by posing as a member of the maintenance team, saying there was a water issue with the apartment upstairs, just in case she was actually there. He never got around to that," Gary said.

DJ moved to the side on the table floor so that he could talk in peace and focus on the conversation. He couldn't believe Gary already had an update.

"Things didn't tank, did they? Was she still there? I was sure she would be gone by now," he said.

"No, she was gone, but my guy didn't get into her apartment. Before he could change into maintenance staff clothing which the maintenance guy got for him, she came through the apartment lobby and she wasn't alone. She was walking briskly and having a shouting match with an older, scruffy looking guy and a woman who looked like she'd lived a hard life, probably from drugs. The woman was carrying an old torn up brown suitcase and the guy was smoking, which the building didn't allow. My guy was top of his game though. He was able to snap some good photos of all three of them as they walked across the lobby to the elevator with the young woman yelling at him to put out his cigarette. She was hollering at him and the older woman was badgering her about needing money and how she wasn't leaving town until she got what she came for. I'm about to text you the pictures. My guy is still there waiting. He followed them up to the floor and listened at her front door. He heard them talking about a large amount of money that was owed to them and how the younger woman had better find a way to pay them or they would make her life a living hell. Those are my guys words. Do you want him to hang around and still try to get in?" Gary asked.

DJ was troubled. He didn't realize Avalon knew anyone other than Jermony and his family and there was no way those people would be linked to him.

"No. Send me the photos and let me get a look at these people," he responded.

"Hold tight."

DJ waited and looked around, smiling at those who passed by him. He knew he looked suspicious standing in one place in all black looking out of place as he paced back and forth, but things were heating up and he felt like he was actually getting someplace. He'd overheard Avalon having a conversation with someone about money and this could be the same people or person.

When his cell vibrated, he quickly checked the photos from the text and without knowing it, he held his breath. It wasn't until seconds later that he realized he needed to keep breathing even through the realization that he recognized the two people in the photo with Avalon. She was with the two strange characters who were seen walking around the casino looking like they were hoping to score without actually playing anything. He had video of them on saved digital stream in his office. What was Avalon doing with people like that. He stared at the pictures coming through and he could see that Avalon was bothered. He felt like he was looking at a woman who was receiving two surprised guests. Who they were to her, he didn't know, but he knew birds of a feather did flock together. They could be people she was hooked up in while in New York who found out she was now in Chicago. He then tossed out that idea remembering that all of the people involved in the sting in New York were much higher caliber than those in these photos with her. Who were they?

"Gary, do you know if she is still in the apartment right now?" DJ asked.

"Hold on a second, let me check with him," Gary replied.

DJ waited a few minutes and then heard Gary clear his throat.

"I pinged him on his cell and he said she is still there. He's no longer outside of her apartment door because he didn't want to draw attention to himself just standing there. He's back in the lobby near the elevators. If they come back down, he will see them. He can follow them if you want," Gary offered.

"Yeah, do that. I need to know if they end up making their way her to the casino. Most of all, I need to know who the two people are with the young woman."

"Wait, my guy just texted saying the young woman just exited the elevator alone. The other two must still be in the apartment. What do you want him to do?"

"I think I know where she's going. I need him to stay on the two others. If they leave, follow them. Listen, I have a plan. I saw those two at the casino while I was viewing overnight streams. I think they could be persuaded to come back and we could possibly get some identification on them. Let me give you some information that he can use. Tell him to hang around the lobby and when he sees them, act like he's working for the apartment complex and he's offering tenants one hundred dollars in free play at the casino if they give an honest review of their experience here. Have him tell them that they have to come to the casino with picture identification. Tell him that in order for them to get the money to play, they have to walk up to the main registration desk on the first floor and ask for Sally. When Sally walks up, they have to say, 'Chicago does it like no other'. That way, Sally will capture their information for me and I can have them checked out. Can he do that?" DJ asked.

"On it. I'll have him offer it when he sees them and I'll text you if they accept. I would suggest telling them that they had one hour to get to the casino in order to get the prize. I'll have him play it up like this is being done all over town. How's that?" Gary asked.

"That'll work."

"What about the young woman who left?"

DJ knew she was probably headed to Jermony's house and he had no concerns there. Once he had information on her two guests, he would deal with her later at his place. He wasn't going to let whatever was going on fester any longer. Chicago would not be another New York. He was betting on himself to get control over whatever was going on before it got out of his hands.

"Don't worry about her for now. It's the seedy looking two-some that I need information on now. I'll be at the casino if you need me. Either you or your guy should text me if it looks like they are going to take him up on the offer. I'll be on this end keeping my eyes out for them," he said.

"Got it. I'll be in touch."

"Listen, any comps I can get you at the casino, let me know. I appreciate you doing this for me and I will be compensating your guy very well."

"I appreciate that. I haven't had a chance to get to the casino yet, but I will soon. I'm leading the security detail for Tucker Glass' fundraiser. I look forward to meeting you then."

"Looking forward to it."

DJ tried his best to control his angry breathing. Avalon wasn't new; she was the same old Justice from New York, but this time, he was ready for her. He was DJ – Black to others, but now a force to be reckoned with for everyone. Not even a sexy body could deter him from shutting her down.

**

After being at Jermony's house for the past two hours, Avalon hadn't figured out a way to either ask him for the money her mother demanded or a way to steal it from his safe. She didn't have the combination and she knew he wasn't going to just give it to her.

After Sunday lunch with him and Kimberly with the kids off to church with Kimberly's mother, the three of them sat around the dining room table where Jermony had arranged for her and Kimberly to get to know each other better. She decided to go for the sympathy vote by telling them about her life growing up with a mother who was on drugs all the time and who drank heavily with one man after another going in and out of their house. She told them of times when she had to pick her mother up from the street outside of their apartment building and drag her inside to the bed that sat on the floor with only a mattress. It's how they both slept at night. When her mother had men over, she had to sleep in the living on an old sofa, trying her best to avoid springs that were making their way through the thin cloth. She spoke of how nasty it was that they'd found the sofa near a dumpster where someone had thrown it out. She had missed many days of school and often didn't have clean clothes to wear. Her friends would bring her clean clothes from their house so that she could change in the bathrooms. No one bothered her and everyone would tell her that she was too pretty to be dirty.

They had talked over food and then over mimosas until she came up with an idea. She would boldly ask Jermony for some money and hoped that he would need to go to the safe to get it.

"Listen, I hate to always seem like I'm coming to you for money, but until I get my first check, I'm a kind of short on money. I was hoping to get cable installed along with internet service and some other essentials. I promise to pay you back when I get my check, but you know I don't start my first day until tomorrow. I hate to ask," Avalon said, making sure she looked as sad and pathetic as she could.

She looked down shyly as if she was even embarrassed to ask, when the truth was, nothing really embarrassed her except for her crazy ass mother who was at the moment, taking over her apartment as if it was hers.

"What? That's not a problem and cable and internet are a

necessity these days. I'll give you some extra so that you don't have to ride out here if you fall short before your first check. Don't worry about it. I keep telling you that we are family and I understand what you've gone through and what it's taking for you to build your life back up. Let me run up to my room real quick and I'll be right back," Jermony said.

As soon as he was gone, Avalon picked up her drink and tried to avoid looking at Kimberly. She already knew the look she would see; one of disgust and questioning.

"I know what you're doing," Kimberly finally said.

Without looking at her, Avalon responded.

"What? I'm not doing anything," she said sheepishly.

"Cut the crap. I'm on to you and soon, Jermony will be too. Cable? Internet? Where is all the money you swindled out of people in New York and other places that we probably don't even know about?" Kimberly asked.

"Why are you so suspicious when Jermony isn't? Are you mad that I could be encroaching on your life? I'm family and Jermony said family helps family," she said.

"True, but you haven't been any help to this family. You seem to keep taking and taking. You hit the jackpot with him turning out to be your brother. I got it – he loves you now that he's found you. I love him with everything in me and I don't want to see him hurt."

Avalon heard her sincerity and she didn't want to hurt Jermony any more than Kimberly wanted to see him hurt, but the alternative would be a lot worse and a lot more embarrassing.

She couldn't explain right now. She needed to get upstairs somehow.

"I have to go to the bathroom. I know there are a few on

this level," she said standing. "I'll be right back."

Before Kimberly could answer, Avalon left the table, taking her purse and her phone with her. She didn't know about Kimberly, but if the shoe was on the other foot, she would go through Kimberly's purse if she left it on the table. It's just how she thought.

When she was out of Kimberly's sight and instead of going to the powder room at the bottom of the spiral, white marble staircase, Avalon removed her high-heels so that they wouldn't make a sound and she tiptoed up the stairs. As she reached their bedroom, Jermony was just finishing up a phone call he must have gotten when he left the table. Lady luck was in her corner because she was just in time to see him put his code in the safe to open it. She quickly took out her cell phone and focused as closely as she could on what he was doing. She smiled when she was able to see all six numbers he entered to get it to open. After the safe was open, she danced inwardly that she now had the code to unlock it and when he opened the door wider, she was thankful that he was one of those rich players who kept a lot of money at home. She saw him take a lot of hundreds from a wrapped stack of bills and she could see a lot more stacks and how far they went back in the safe. She also saw some jewelry and other items. She wouldn't touch that, but the money, he wouldn't miss if she took stacks from the back. She bet he didn't even know exactly how much he had and didn't care since he had millions. Only people without money keep track of every cent. At least that was her belief.

As Jermony closed the safe, his cell phone rang again and she quietly went back down the hall and down the steps. As she walked down, Kimberly came around the corner and stood at the bottom of the steps.

"You must have forgotten there were several bathrooms on this level and you didn't have to go upstairs," Kimberly said questionably.

Avalon played it off.

"I know. I was hoping to catch Jermony to tell him I may not need as much as he thought I did. I was listening to you and you're right that I've only been taking. I only need a small amount," she lied.

"Oh, is that so. Well, did you tell him?" she asked.

"No, he was on his cell phone so I came back down."

"And I see you took off your shoes. The floors are marble. You didn't have to do that," Kimberly continued on suspiciously grilling and eyeing her. Avalon recognized a woman who knew a hustle when she was one.

"I did. I wasn't sure. I wanted to respect your house and not walk up in my shoes, especially with the kids and all. I didn't want to bring outside germs from my shoes to the bedroom level. I was thinking of you," Avalon said, walking past Kimberly back into the dining room. "Speaking of you – if you and Jermony need a date night, I can come watch the kids one day this week. I know you don't see each other with him being on the road and I bet you'd like a night out, maybe at the casino. I'm hoping to bond with my nieces and nephew and I'm free every evening this week. Think about it. I'm trying to help and not just take. See, I'm already trying to learn from you and take your advice.

"Did you forget you needed to use the bathroom?"

Avalon turned and walked by her to the powder room.

"Nope, was going to put my shoes back on first, but that can wait. I'm sure your floors are sparkling and shining and definitely clean enough for me to walk on with my bare feet. You know, with this mansion and all the money you have to pay people to keep it all shiny and new."

Without any more reaction, Avalon went into the bathroom and slammed the door.

**

Kimberly walked back into the dining room and sat down. She knew that Jermony had on blinders when it came to Avalon, but she didn't and she had a feeling of what Avalon was all about, even if Jermony couldn't see it. Speaking of her husband, she turned when he jogged into the room.

"Where is Avie?" he asked.

"I see you got her some money from the safe," she said.

"I did. I want to be sure she has enough to not have to worry about anything. We have plenty."

"You need to think before you just keep handing over money like this, especially these large bills. I know you want to do so much for her, but just be careful. I know she's your sister and you waited a long time to find her and the others. Everything is not what it seems and you're too open when it comes to her. She offered to babysit for us one night this week so that we can have a date night."

"That's nice. The kids love her already and they would love having an evening of fun with their aunt. You wouldn't have to call a sitter and your mother can get a break from doing it. I think we should take her up on it. I want to have her around and know that she has us."

Kimberly stood and walked over to him after he sat down at the table and placed the money in front of the seat where Avalon was sitting. She could see at least two-grand, maybe three. She loved how generous her husband could be, but she didn't want to see him taken advantage of or to see his connection with his sister turn out to be a bad end after he spent so much time and money on finding her.

Leaning down, she wrapped her arms around his neck, kissed him on the cheek and whispered in his ear.

"Date night is on and before we go, change the passcode on the safe. You'll thank me later."

She walked back to her seat, not needing to look at the state of shock she knew his face was in. She didn't need to explain because being married to him for eight years, he understood. What he didn't know was that he was not only protecting him, she was protecting Avalon, to her dismay.

12

DJ was furious. He'd spent his entire day focused on the antics of Avalon Hart and what he was able to find out by way of the many resources he had in law enforcement only angered him more.

After hearing from Gary that the two people who were seen with Avalon had come down on the elevator in her apartment building and had taken the casino offer bait, he waited patiently for them to arrive. He was told the couple quickly found a cab and hustled to get to the casino in record speed for their one hundred dollars in gaming credit. Gary's guy was able to follow them in his car and the moment they pulled up to the casino, DJ got a text that they had arrived.

He had already school Sally, one of the front registration desk clerks on what she needed to do. DJ made sure he stayed out of sight. He didn't want anyone from security to spook them as they had during their first visit to the casino.

He watched from a good vantage point as both handed their identification to Sally who then captured everything and issued them their credits to play. Within seconds of practically having cash on hand, he watched them race off to the gaming floor. He knew they couldn't care about surveying their experience and DJ didn't care. He only wanted information on who they were.

As he walked around his apartment, waiting on Avalon to confront her, he played over in his mind what he was able to find out.

The woman was Virginia Hart from Raleigh, North Carolina and to his surprise, she was Avalon's mother. The guy was Reginald Moore, a man with a long criminal past of drug possession, theft, burglary and armed robbery. He had even been charged with assault a few times. Avalon's mother's record wasn't much shorter. She had a lot of charges that dealt with abandoning Avalon as a child along with drug arrests, public disorderly and indecency charges along with assault and battery charges. Both had small stints in jail, but nothing lengthy. There was no doubt in his mind that them being in Chicago was for no good reason at all and the fact that not only did he hear Avalon talking about money with them, but Gary's guy did as well. What did Avalon owe that she had to pay up for? Virginia was her mother? What did she have on Avalon that made her indebted to her? What kind of mother does that? If Avalon owed her a large sum of money, his concern was what she was going to do to get it and did it have anything to do with the casino. Tonight, he would find out.

He needed a solid, common sense thinker to talk to and he tried reaching him earlier at the casino, but Torrence had been off-sight meeting with a team of people about his next big casino venture. When he sent him a text that they needed to talk, Torrence told him he would call him, but he hadn't heard back. He was growing more nervous as time got closer to Avalon arriving. He needed to talk to Torrence beforehand considering something going down could involve the casino. In his mind, he couldn't imagine Avalon by herself coming through with some scheme to defraud the casino, but he couldn't put it past her. What she did in New York was still fresh on his mind.

He took out his phone and called Torrence again and this time, he answered.

"Aw, man – I forgot to call you back," Torrence exclaimed.

DJ didn't even have to say anything before Torrence and he hoped he was still intruding.

"Did I catch you at a bad time?" DJ asked.

"No. I'm in my car heading home at a decent hour for a change. Reese and I are planning a quiet evening at home. With our schedules, we don't get to do that too often. I know you reached out earlier and I got caught up in some business. What's going on? What's so urgent?" he asked.

Pausing before spilling, DJ knew the conversation was going to be a hard one. He didn't want to hear a bunch of 'I told you so' statements from anyone, especially not Torrence or his sister.

"It's Avalon. I think she's up to something," he said.

"Something like what?" Torrence asked.

"Something that might involve the casino. I've caught her in a sneaky lie and all day, I've been chasing that lie with the help of a friend of yours and Reese's – the security specialist, Gary. He helped me do some checking and I think Avalon is up to old tricks and she's brought them here to

Chicago. Now, I can't say it directly involves the casino, but I don't know what to do with the information I have. Do I let her attempt to follow through with whatever she is planning? Do I confront her and give her a chance to explain herself? Do I go to the police, though I don't have enough to warrant their involvement? I'm trying to protect the casino in case it's a part of something, but I just don't know," he said.

"What do you have on her?"

"Well, we were in bed and she left out when she thought I was asleep and I overheard a call she was on about a large sum of money," he began explaining.

"Wait, what? You and Avalon were in bed? You're sleeping with her again? When did all of this happen?" Torrence asked.

DJ forgot that he hadn't told anyone about his hooking back up with Avalon on an intimate level. It sort of just fell into his own lap and he didn't think to share that with others.

"Yeah, that happened and it's been about a week now," he admitted.

"Dude! Are you serious right now?" Torrence exclaimed

"I know, again I'm thinking with the wrong head, but it just sort of happened, but now that it has, I've been making sure I am aware of what she's doing and not brushing anything under the table. Remember you got the digital streams and one of the couples that were pointed out is actually Avalon's crooked mother and her criminal boyfriend. They are here from North Carolina and Avalon hasn't said anything about them. I think they are planning something and it may not be only the three of them. For now, they are all I have. Her mother is talking about a large sum of money that Avalon owes her and she's here to collect, almost as if it's some kind of bribe. I don't know what it is. I'm waiting on Avalon now. I was going to confront her with what she's been keeping from me, but what if this is much bigger like in New York? What if I tip the hand of someone bigger than her behind this and she's again small-fry?"

"Okay, DJ, exhale brother. You don't seem to be breathing between words. If you and Avalon have grown close again, then talk to her. You weren't able to do that back in New York and you regretted that you didn't know enough back then to stop her, but now you do. It sounds like her mother may have something on her and Avalon may be caught up, but not of her own doing. I could be wrong too, but if you're hooking back up with her, I know it's not just about the sex with you because you care about her. Trust your instincts and talk to her and see if she will explain it all. You'll know if what you feel is real and if her feelings for you are real. You know what to do if this thing is big and we have the best security team on this coast, so I'm not concerned about the casino. We've had bigger fish try their hands and we've always come out on top. Remember, I always bet on Black. I trust you know what to do. Call me if you need me. If you care about her or even love her, try to help her before you persecute her. I think she's had enough of people doing that. I had lunch with Jermony last week and he shared some things about her life that made me think she has had a real hard go at life and all she needs is people who really care about her to have her back. I don't think she's ever had that," Torrence said.

"I want to protect and help her, but I can't if she doesn't let me in."

"That's why you let her talk and rather than threaten her

police or jail, find out if what's she's involved in can use some help. We're all here, me, Reese, her brother and the rest of our crew. You need us, call us," Torrence said.

"I got to go. A text from her just came over my phone that she's parking her car. I'll hit you back later if I need you," DJ said.

"Bro, just remember, she's from a different cloth than you or me and she's had a lot of struggles that no twenty-five-year-old should ever have. Hustling may have always been her way, but it's not her only way. If you care about her, come from that angle of help and love and I think she'll open up to you. I don't know all the details, but it sounds like her mother is holding all the keys and Avalon may be getting hustled. Watch your back. I'm betting on you, Black."

DJ hung up just as he heard Avalon knocking on the door. When he opened it, she leaped into his arms so fast that he didn't know what to do other than to stand there and hold her tight. He couldn't sense that she was crying, but that she definitely needed his hug. He was upset with her, but he loved her and she needed him.

"What's wrong?" he asked when he tried to pull away, but she held on to him tighter. He couldn't even shut the door because they hadn't moved enough away from it. When she didn't answer, he let her have what she needed he just stood there and pulled her even tighter to him.

"Avalon? Talk to me. What's wrong?" he asked again.

"My life is all kinds of messed up and I don't know what to do," she said.

She was coming to him before he could bring his suspicions up to her. He wasn't prepared for that. He was ready to grill her like an episode of Perry Mason, an old court television series he still loved to watch on cable.

Finally, moving, he closed and locked the door behind them and when he looked into her face, which he missed when he opened the door because she had leaped right at him, he saw that she had been crying. Her makeup was smeared and she didn't look like herself. She was impeccably dressed like usual, but she stood as if the life had been drained out of her body.

"Talk to me. What's going on? You didn't mention anything on the phone when we talked thirty minutes ago. You were your usual chipperly self. What happened?" he asked, walking her over to his sofa and sitting down next to her.

"You're going to hate me and never want to see me again and I don't want that. I love you, DJ. I did in New York when I hurt you and didn't mean to. I never stopped loving you. I knew you were here in Chicago and when Jermony asked me again about moving here after everything went down, I took him up on it. I knew I would see you. I couldn't stop thinking about all that I had done to you. I'd never, ever had anyone care about me the way that you did and I knew I blew that out of the water. I lied when I told you I didn't know you were here. I'm sorry about that," she said.

DJ saw tears falling from her eyes and his heart dropped. He reached and wiped them away, but found they were falling quicker than he could wipe.

"Why would I hate you and never want to see you about that? It's a little white lie and nothing major. Not enough to warrant these tears," he said.

"That, that's not all," she cried.

"Avalon, you have to stop crying and tell me what's going

on. I can't help you if you don't talk to me," he said.

When she looked up at him, he smiled.

"You mean that don't you? You really mean it when you say you would help me. I knew that back in New York. I knew that if I told you that you would help me, but I didn't I let you get wrapped up in it when I could have saved you by coming clean. I can't do that to you again. I can't," she proclaimed.

"You can't do what?"

"I can't keep things from you again. I know we've only been together a week, but it's been heavenly. I feel like I can really get my life on a good path, but evil keeps creeping in and I can't get a leg up. I'm so lost right now."

"Calm down and talk to me."

DJ was glad that he didn't have to confront her with accusations. It seems she really does want to do better by coming to him before he hit her with what he knew. He would let her have the floor.

"My mother is in Chicago and it's not for anything good. She's here demanding a large sum of money from me; money I don't have. I found a way to get it, but I can't do that to my brother. He's done so much for me and I was planning on stealing from him. I even got the code to the safe in his house earlier today. I went there to figure out a way to get the money my mother is asking for and I could only think of getting it from him. I couldn't ask him for that amount and I figured with all the money he has, he had to keep a lot of it in the house and he did. I was going to go back, babysit the kids this week after I offered to give him and Kimberly a date night out while I watch them. I was going to take money from his safe and I knew he wouldn't miss it because he had a lot of it in there. I think Kimberly was suspicious of me and when I got in my car to leave, I sat on the road outside of their house about a block away and I just cried. I was back in the hot seat, stealing and conniving and I was about to do that to my own brother; my own flesh and blood. I was becoming my mother. She's an evil person. I know I have never talked about her to you, but she is pure evil and I'm turning into her," Avalon lamented.

DJ's heart went out to her. He knew Avalon wasn't evil. She'd just never had anyone who cared enough to be in her corner. Torrence was right. She needed him and the rest of their gang more than she needed him to scold and accuse her.

"Okay, what did you do after that and how does this tie to your mother? What does she have that she is using to get that kind of money out of you?" he asked.

"Oh, I don't want to tell you this. You'll never look at me the same. You'll never want to touch me or love me again. I'm dirty. I've done some horrible, disgusting things that I don't want to come out. My mother is threatening to do just that if I don't get her the money she's asking for. I made the mistake, back in New York, of telling her about Jermony and she knows he's rich. She's bee blackmailing me to get money from him. I was going to do whatever I needed to do in order to get the money to get her off of my back, but then I realized she was never going to stop coming back for more. I would never be free from her clutches," she said.

DJ took her hands in his to try and calm her down. He could tell he was rattled and he wanted nothing more than to help her especially if her mother was holding something over her head.

"What does she have? You have to tell me. I promise I

won't judge you or criticize or turn away from you. I love you, Avalon. Like you, I fell in love with you in New York and I've still carried that torch for you. I love that you're coming to me this time before you do something that could bring trouble in your life again and stealing from Jermony could make the one person who is actually family and loves you, hate you and turn away from you. Talk to me, baby."

He waited for her to gather her words, giving her the time she needed to face him with what was terrorizing her life from the past.

"When I was young, like around ten years old, my mother sold me to men for drugs and money. It went on until I was around fourteen years old. it was a horrible, horrible time in my life and I had no control over it. She would hold me down while men did terrible things to me. She would cover my mouth to keep me from screaming and then would threaten me with telling everyone what I was doing with these men if I told anyone what was happening. Some of the men took pictures and video of what they did to me. When I was fifteen, a man my mother was seeing brought two friends over to the house and I had had enough of what she was letting men do to me. She screamed at me to go into the bedroom and get undressed and to wait and she would send them in one at a time. I ran into the bedroom, grabbed some clothes and jumped out of our second-floor window. I hurt my leg very bad, but my determination to get away was stronger than the pain. I ran and ran and stayed from one place to another where friends would let me crash with them at night after their parents had gone to bed. For years after that, I did what I could to survive. I stole from people and business, I conned people, I panhandled. I did a lot of things, but I never, ever prostituted myself. After what my mother did, I never, ever did that. I didn't want a man touching me. When I turned seventeen, I ran into my mother again and she apologized saying she was sick, but was all better. I was alone in the world and had no one. All I ever wanted was my mother's love and I resolved to get it by any means necessary. We started running scams together from everything I learned about being on the streets. I didn't go back to staying with her, but we stayed connected. I thought the things I was doing would get her to love me, but she never really did. She only wanted to take from me and I learned to take from others. I was willing to take from my own brother to satisfy her disgusting greed. I couldn't let her release those photos of me to the press. She was going to tout them using Jermony as the draw to gain attention since he's my brother. She wanted to embarrass me and make me lose him as a brother and she hoped it would destroy him in the press also. I couldn't have that. I also couldn't hurt him or you. I wanted to be so much more in life now. I have Jermony, I have you and I love you and I wanted to be much more for you. I wanted to prove that I wasn't a lowlife living in beautiful skin. I have a good heart. I swear I do," Avalon pleaded.

When she cried hard, DJ picked her up and sat her across his lap and let her cry it out. He needed her to release all the hurt, anger, frustration and low self-esteem she was holding on to. He was holding in his own anger and rage at what her mother tried to do and what she had done to her as a little girl. He wasn't disgusted by Avalon, but by what her mother was attempting to do. He already knew he was going to need some help, but he needed her to be open to the help, which mean telling Jermony what was going on. He was family and Avalon needed to know how real family has each other's backs.

"Baby, listen to me. Cry it all out the way you need to. We can sit here all night and I'll hold you while you do that. I'm not going anywhere. I love you, I will continue to love you and nothing you can say will turn me away from you. I'm glad you came to me. I know your mother is in town. I was going to ask you about her. You were acting strange when I asked you if you were talking to someone the other night and you lied when I knew the truth. I was cautious and had someone doing a little checking and he saw you with your mother and Reginald at your building. I ran a scam of my own to get information on them and they fell for it and of course it involved money."

When Avalon leaned up, he thought she would get out of his lap in anger that he'd checked up on her, but she didn't.

"You did what? Why?" she asked.

"Because I didn't want to see you get into any more trouble. I heard you on the phone and I knew she was holding something over you, though I didn't know at the time that it was your mother. Now that I do, that's even worse. She won't get away with it. I'm here and I'll protect you. You have to tell Jermony. If you really love and trust him and believes that he loves you, you will tell him the truth. No more lies. No more schemes. Your mother is not worth the ground she walking on or the air she's breathing after what she has done and is doing to you. One thing I do know is that, if she does anything with those photos or videos of you as a child, it's call child pornography and she'll go to jail. Do you have any voicemails or notes or anything where she's blackmailing you and you have it as proof?" he asked.

"Yes. I have lots of voicemails where she says she's going to sell photos of me as a child having sex with grown men. She even says that she didn't get enough money from those men by selling me and now she needs more to keep quiet about it."

"That will all help. Listen, I'm glad you came to me about this. There is no need to hurt anymore. I'm here for you. Jermony is here for you and so are my sister and her boyfriend, Torrence. We can help you, but you have to be open and honest with us."

"Okay. I want to do that. I want to get away from my old life. I like this new one with you much better. I'm starting a new job tomorrow. I have my own place and I want a better life. I love you," Avalon said.

"I love you, too, baby. Let's call Jermony and see if we can pay him a visit tonight. WE need to get this dealt with. I'm also going to reach out to a friend named Gary who also works in security and law enforcement. I think he could help put an end to this. Are you game?" he asked.

"Yes, I am."

Avalon stood from his lap and searched for her phone. He sat still and let her do what she needed to do. They were putting an end to her old life and getting rid of old evil so that it never reared its ugly head in their lives again.

"Jermony, it's me. Can DJ and I come see you tonight? We need to talk to you and it's important."

DJ smiled. He was seeing a new side to Avalon and he knew everything was going to be alright as soon as he helped her drop some old baggage.

13

Jermony sat stunned and DJ didn't blame him. As he looked around the table from Avalon who was crying, to Kimberly who was practically doubled over with tears and then to Jermony who appeared so angry that he was worried about the plans to harm Avalon's mother and her boyfriend that were running through his mind. He could see the wheels turning.

"That crazy bitch!" Jermony hollered and stood up so fast, the dining room chair crashed to the floor. No one moved to pick it up as tempers ran high after Avalon told them all everything. She'd even shared more that she had left out when they talked before coming out to Jermony's house to bring him up to speed. DJ knew there was enough hurt to go around along with love and support for Avalon. None of them could have known what her life was like and where she thought they would turn away from her, there was more love than had been there before they arrived.

"Oh, my god! What kind of monster is she? I have babies

and I can't begin to imagine the horror you went through," Kimberly said.

Before anyone could answer, Kimberly leaped out of her seat and went around and pulled Avalon into the kind of hug that could only be described as loving and devotion.

"I'm going to kill her!" Jermony shouted.

DJ stood and walked over to him, trying to calm him down. He had his own murderous thoughts when it came to Avalon's mother, but they had to pull it back. Avalon didn't need this right now. He turned to Gary for help with calming Jermony down.

"Look, tempers are high right now. What your sister shared was a lot and has caused emotions to be all over the place, but level heads need to prevail. We need to bring in the authorities and I can take care of that for you. Avalon, do you know where these pictures and videos are of you? Does she have them with her?" Gary asked.

"No. She always talked about some locker at a gym back in her neighborhood, but I never knew which one. I've only seen the pictures once and that was before I moved to New York to get away from her. She still found me and the threats continued. I've been giving her money for years and it's never been enough. All that I did to get money was to keep her quiet. I may have benefited with just enough to survive, but most of it went to her – even the money from my brother."

Avalon stood and walked over to and DJ held her in his arms with her back to him as she spoke to Jermony directly.

"I'm sorry I thought about stealing from you. I'm so sorry. I didn't know what to do. If I asked you for it, I would have to tell you why and I was ashamed of what I did," she said.

When Avalon lowered her head, DJ lifted it back up with his hands and leaned down to her ear.

"No more hanging your head in shame. There will never be a reason for you to hang your head low," he said and kissed her on the cheek, showing her that he was right there with her.

"DJ is right. Don't be ashamed of what happened to you. That was in no way your fault. Your mother was supposed to protect you, not sell you like you were nothing. That's not real family behavior. We'll deal with this with Gary's help. She's been blackmailing you all this time and now she's here in Chicago? On my turf? Oh, it's on. I want to see her in jail! No getting her off or letting her walk away. We need to see to it that she goes down for what she's done to Avie and for what she's trying to do now. What can we do?" Jermony asked Gary.

"Jermony, let DJ and I handle this. We need you to stay clear of this. There is no need to get the media involved and the way they love all aspects of your life, this, I want to be sure doesn't get out. The plan I have in mind will make sure none of this ever surfaces. I will need Avalon to call her mother and tell her that she has the money, but first she'll need to make sure the pictures and videos actual exist. I'm going to reach to law enforcement sources I have to get them on board, but the plan I have I believe will work. Once we have that evidence in hand and it has her mother's finger prints on it, then I think we'll be able to have her picked up. Avalon, you said the pictures are somewhere in North Carolina, but you don't know where?" Gary asked.

"Yes."

"I need to fly to North Carolina," DJ said.

"No!" Avalon shouted and turned to him. You can't see those pictures of me like that," she cried.

"Baby, I have no intentions of looking at anything like that. I'm sickened at the thought of it, not of you, but of a mother who would do such a thing. I don't want that stuff in anyone else's hands. Tell your mother that she will need to get the pictures and video and show them to you to know that they exist and you will give her double the money if she gives them to you and leaves you alone. Is there anything else we need besides the recordings you have of her blackmailing you that we need to know about? Law enforcement will need all of that," DJ said.

"Wait! Yes. I saw some of one of the videos once and you can hear my mother on them telling me to shut up and take it because rent was due. I think she's even captured in one as she's holding me down. She showed it to me once to make sure I never told anyone," she said.

"I want to bury her deep!" DJ exclaimed.

"Stand in line!" Jermony shouted.

"How will she get the stuff if she's here in Chicago?" Kimberly asked. "How do we get her back to North Carolina?"

"Part of the deal is for her to produce what she has. We can get her a plane ticket back, courtesy of Avalon and have her watched by authorities. I want to be there to see it all go down and make sure she's in custody. I don't want any slipups. She needs to go down for this," DJ said.

"Promise me you won't get yourself into any trouble. Let law enforcement handle her and Reggie. They can be slick," Avalon said.

"I'm reaching out to my contacts at the bureau to set up a meeting tomorrow and to have them bring agents on the line from North Carolina to prepare."

"You can't go back to your place if your mother and that guy are there. You can stay here at the house with us," Kimberly said. "I'll have a room made up for you," she added.

"I want to stay with DJ until he leaves. I need to be with him," Avalon explained. "I know you and Jermony are here for me and I love you both for that. I will come here when DJ leaves for North Carolina. Wait, I have to work tomorrow. I have training as a new employee," she said.

"I'll call Torrence. Don't worry about that. For now, we want to keep you safe. Tell your mother you're staying with your boyfriend and she and Reggie can have the place to themselves tonight. We will connect with Gary's contacts tomorrow and see how fast we can get them on a plane and back to North Carolina. As soon as I hear they are going to go for it, I'll catch an earlier flight and have them tracked until I get there," DJ said.

"Promise me you'll be safe. Nothing can happen to you. I wouldn't survive if it did. Promise me!" Avalon shouted and went back into his arms.

"Baby, I promise I will be safe and as soon as this is over and your mother is in custody, I'm coming right back here to you. Gary, lay out for us what Avalon needs to say and do and tomorrow, we work them the way they've been working my baby here all these years," DJ said.

Everyone nodded and sat around the table as Gary laid out his idea for how it should all go down.

DJ settled back with Avalon sitting on his lap. He held her tight with promises that he would make her life better from this moment on. He smiled knowing that he was about to help Avalon get a clean slate in life – a new chance to finally be free from her past.

"Are you listening, DJ?" Gary asked.

"Yeah, I am. I was just thinking that Virginia Hart must be one of those people who bets on red when she should have been betting on black to win because she is about to become the biggest loser."

They all cheered when Jermony pumped his fist in the air.

14
One Week Later

DJ stepped into the shower after arriving home from his flight to North Carolina and was happy to find Avalon in his bed. He had called her first after everything went down and he felt comfortable that all of the news he had was good news. As the hot water cascaded down his back, DJ tried to let the water wash away the vileness that is Avalon's mother. He'd never met a more hateful woman who was unhappy with her own life and who was hell-bent on ruining anyone else's life who had a little bit of happiness. He was glad that Avalon would never have to live under her thumb again and those pictures and videos would be destroyed after her mother went to court. Because of the blackmailing and by her own admissions of what she'd done, Virginia Hart was going to go to jail for a long time. Her boyfriend had outstanding warrants and it looked like he was going away for a long time too because the lockbox where the pictures and videos on old cell phones were kept was registered in his name and his fingerprints were found all over the photos. He had knowledge and had them in his possession, so he was being charge too. DJ didn't care what happened to either of them as long as he could get them out of Avalon's life so that she could move on and prosper.

After leaving Jermony's house that night, he and Avalon had stayed up talking and for the first time since they reconnected, they didn't feel the need to make love. He wanted to hold her in his arms and let her sleep peacefully for the first time in years. The next day, he called Torrence and told him all that was happening and Torrence assured him that Avalon's job would be there when everything calmed down and was figured out. He wanted to be a part of her finding her footing in life. After he and Avalon got dressed, they met up with Gary for breakfast who gave them the rundown of what was next. Avalon told them that her mother had called her late the night before and she did what they told her to do. She told her mother that she was able to get the money from Jermony's safe and that she would give her double if she gave her the pictures and the videos. Money-hungry Virginia saw dollar signs when she thought of having two-hundred-thousand instead of one-hundred-thousand. Avalon offered to get her and Reggie round-trip tickets to and from North Carolina. She agreed to give her ten thousand dollars and promised to show her pictures of the rest of the money if she got on a plane the next day and got the pictures. Her mother jumped all over that.

After meeting with Gary and getting the ten grand from Jermony, who didn't care if he got it back, he just wanted Avalon safe, they met with the local Chicago branch of the FBI. After that, DJ took a private jet, courtesy of Jermony, to North Carolina and waited with the North Carolina office of the FBI for Virginia and Reggie to land later that evening.

The plan was in place.

Once they followed them to the box that had the pictures, Virginia and Reggie were arrested as they took the large dirty brown envelope from the box. When they turned around, law enforcement snatched them up and it wasn't an easy take-down. Though Reggie didn't resist, Virginia fought with all of her might and for a meek and frail woman, she was strong. It took several agents to get her on the ground and even then, she flailed about so wildly that they had to use a taser to calm her down enough to get handcuffs on her. As she was being dragged away, because she wouldn't use her legs to stand, DJ had looked at her and told her to always bet on Black and he meant it. He had spent a whole week in North Carolina getting as much information as he could. Mid-week, Gary joined him to see if there was anything he could help with. Gary, using his contacts, was able to keep information flowing in DJ's direction and as he found out what was going on, he called Avalon and Jermony to let them know. He was thankful that she stayed the week with her brother. He didn't want her to be alone in her place. When she told him how dirty and disgusting her mother had left her place after only one day in it, he told her to never go back there. He wanted her to move in with him or get another place. He was happy when she said she wanted to be with him. He told her to get his extra key from his sister and that Reese would help her move her things in while he was away.

When the week wound down and he knew Virginia wasn't going anywhere and wouldn't be bothering Avalon anymore, DJ took a flight back to Chicago and raced to get home to Avalon. It was after midnight when he arrived because he stopped by the casino to check on things. He had talked to Avalon right before his flight took off and she told him she was going to take a bath and wait up for him. He told her to get some rest because they had years and years to wait up for each other. He smiled when she told him that Reese helped her add a woman's touch to his place and she hoped he would like it. He told her that it was their place together and he already knew he would love it because she would be there with him.

After leaving the casino, he finally rushed home and moved about quietly after discovering Avalon fast asleep in bed. He kissed her sweetly on the lips and quietly moved to the shower to wash off the stink of the week in North Carolina in hopes that the water would remove the idea of what Avalon had gone through. He was still hurting for her and wished he could remove the memories of that time in her life from her mind. He'd spoken to Reese while at the airport in North Carolina where he wanted to cry himself, but he held strong. He wanted to be strong for Avalon, but most of all, he needed to know how to help her. Reese told him that he needed to convince Avalon to talk to a professional and maybe the two of them could talk with one together as a couple. Avalon had a lot of healing to do and they also needed to heal together with what he now knew about her life. He felt good when Reese told him how proud she was of how he stepped in and took care of things. Before he could say his famous line, she said it first. She always counted on *Black!* She cheered even louder for him when he told her that he stopped at an upscale store he found in North Carolina and bought himself a white shirt and he was wearing it on the plane ride home. If Avalon was starting out new, he wanted newness too. He still loved his black attire, but he wanted to add some brightness to their lives and he was even open to discussing their father. He realized he couldn't help Avalon heal if he wasn't willing to heal the damaged parts of his own life and that started with his relationship with their father. Enough time had passed. Now was the time for healing for them all.

As he leaned forward with his hands against the white tiled shower wall, DJ was startled when the shower door opened. He also smiled because he knew that meant his woman was up and when she touched his back with her soft hands, he was not up to, in more ways than one. When she stepped inside and closed the shower door behind her, he turned around and greeted her with a delicious kiss, one he'd been waiting to get since the moment he landed.

"My hero is home!" Avalon exclaimed.

"Hi, baby! I've missed you," he said and pulled her naked body closer to his, allowing her to feel his strong and power love for her and not just because he was aroused, but because his heart was beating hard and fast for her. He took her hand and placed it over his chest so that she could feel it.

"I love you," Avalon whispered.

"You already know, baby. We are love," he replied.

"You didn't wake me when you got home. I heard the shower running and came in."

DJ moaned when she rubbed her hands all up and down his body.

"I'm glad you did. I know you needed your rest. My sister said you were worried about me all week. I told you I would be fine."

"I know. I just wanted you to be fine back here in Chicago and not in that horrible place where I grew up. It's an awful place," she said.

"You're safe here with me now and I'll never, ever let anything or anyone hurt you in any kind of way again," he acknowledged.

"Reese said the same thing. She called me her sister yesterday and I burst out in tears. I've never felt so love in my life than I have since the moment I met you and found out I had a brother. The love has been growing since then. Even Kimberly likes me. She's picking me up tomorrow for a spa day with her, Reese, Sienna and Dexter's wife Alyssa. They told me that I am one of them now and that I will never, ever be alone in this world again. I can't tell you how amazing that sounds!"

"I'm glad you let me in. I'm glad you let us all in. Your life will be nothing like it was and if you need or want anything, all you have to do is tell Black all about it," DJ said and laughed. "Wait – guess what?" he asked.

When Avalon leaned back, she smiled at how big his smile was.

"What?" she asked

"I had on a white shirt today and that's no joke. I bought it before I flew out. It was the first time in years that I didn't wear a black shirt. I liked it."

"So, we can't call you Black anymore?" she asked.

"Baby, you can call me whatever you want," he answered.

"Well, how about my lover-man. I like how that sounds."

"That's music to my ears."

"Well then, can you actually be my lover-man right this second. I've waited a week for you to come home to love me. I've missed you so much. I know we have a lot to talk about and we can do that tomorrow. Tonight, I just want to feel. I just want you all around me. Nothing but you," Avalon moaned out.

Without any pretense, DJ picked her up and turned her around until her back was against the wall.

"I aim to please, baby," he said.

In the next second, DJ opened her legs and slid home. As his mouth covered hers, he poured more than a kiss into the kiss. He poured from his heart the love that overflowed from it. Where they would usually kiss wildly and zestfully, he slowed things down. The kiss was deep and penetratingly slow. He allowed their tongues to mate and know what forever felt like. There would never be another for him or for her – it would from this day forward be them and one day when they got married, which he intends to make happen, and they have kids, they will spread their love out as far as it need to go to make sure their kids feel the love and adoration that Avalon now understood because she now had what she wanted and needed; she had unconditional love.

Moving his hips slowly, he loved her. The water had cooled, but they didn't care. The heat of their skin kept them warm. He held on to Avalon's legs to steady her as her arms encircled his neck. Their moans grew louder as his thrusts grew more determined. Never again would he have to be without this kind of love. He'd found it in New York, lost it and now had it again and it was his for keeps. He was hers for keeps.

Planting his feet firmly on the floor of the shower, he used his powerful legs to hold them up while he rocked her hips up and down on the wall behind them, letting her ride him until she drew every bit of love from him that she needed. This wasn't just sex with them anymore – this was pure, unadulterated, unconditional, untamed, love.

As their breaths quickened, DJ increased the speed, rapidly bringing them to the brink, yet pulling them back when he felt they were reaching their peak.

"Stop," Avalon groaned. "I need to feel it. I'm so close and you keep pulling me back. Love me, baby," she crooned in his ear.

"Hold on, baby."

With that DJ soared into her and in the next instant, they shared a mutual release as the world opened up and their love poured out. He leaned his head down on her shoulder and groaned through a powerful orgasm that rocked him to the core. With Avalon screaming his name again and again, her heard violin sounds in her words and wanted to forever hear her call his name in love. When she shouted, Delvin, he loved her harder. To her, he would be whomever she needed and right now, that's who she needed. She needed the man himself, not a nickname or a persona, she just needed Delvin.

"I love you, so much," Avalon shouted before he captured her lips and mated with her.

"I love you," he shouted and when he felt her body moving on him again as if she was rising for another powerful release, he let go again and came with a force that caused his legs to stiffen and his entire being exploded. Rockets went off in his head, stars were seen behind his closed eye lids as they again, together went with the crashing waves of their love, rising higher and higher where the cares of the natural world no longer existed. They had found a place where only the two of them existed and DJ knew he couldn't wait to go to that place again and again, but only with her.

She called him her hero, but she was his superwoman. She had survived so much and still found a place inside her of where love lived.

As his body calmed and he held her close to him as she peppered his face with kiss after kiss after kiss, he was thankful that he knew to always bet on Black. Black always wins!

Epilogue
Two Months Later
Political Fundraiser

DJ and Reese sat at their table after Councilman Tucker Glass' announcement that Carter Garrison agreed to be his campaign manager. The crowd had gone crazy in the three thousand seat event hall at the casino. The festivities were winding down and people milled about. With Avalon moving about with Jermony as he introduced her to everyone he knew, he watched how she beamed like a brand new, shiny car. It didn't hurt that he knew she was the most beautiful person in the room in a golden yellow evening gown that had to have been made specifically for her. People were complimenting his lady all night long, but no one was doing so more than he was. He wanted to steal her away to a private area and have his way with her, but he could wait until they got home.

"Tonight, was something, huh?" Reese asked.

"It was and this was a huge boost in campaign funds for him. I understand he's already the front-runner to win it all the way," DJ said.

"That's what every poll says and one thing I've known for a long time is that the people love him. Even after getting divorced and that whole mess with his celebrity ex-wife, he is still landing on top."

"I noticed he came alone tonight. He's still not seeing anyone? I know the media has been trying to link him to this woman and that woman, but he hasn't claimed anyone to have on his arm," DJ inquired.

"I asked Sienna about that since she and Carter are close to him. She said that she hasn't heard about a special woman, but that she overheard him talking to his security guy about making sure some woman got home and he would see her later tonight. Carter asked me what I knew and I didn't have a clue. There are a lot of single women here tonight, so it could be any of them. Speaking of single women, did you see our sister? She looks amazing! I'm telling you, there is something going on with her. When have you known her to come to any kind of fundraiser?" Reese asked as she leaned over toward DJ as they both searched the crowd for Nichelle.

"Yeah, and she has disappeared again after acting all mysterious the entire night. She got her hair blown out and I didn't even know her hair was that long and luscious. That navy gown was flawless. I thought she came because of mommy, but she said she didn't know Nichelle was coming either and she missed dinner last Sunday with some excuse about a furniture delivery at the townhouse she shares with her sorority sisters from college. What company delivers on Sunday?" DJ asked.

"Right. Let's find her and ask, but first, here comes your beautiful girlfriend."

DJ stood as Avalon approached. He leaned down for a quick, sweet kiss of her lips.

"Hey, baby. Having a good time?" he asked.

"I'm having the best time. A friend of Jermony's asked me about my makeup and I told her I did it myself. She asked if I could do her makeup for a photoshoot. I think she's a model or something. Isn't that exciting?" she asked.

"Well, you said you wanted to get into cosmetology and also be an esthetician. I've told you that you are a master when it comes to makeup," Reese said. "I've gotten compliments about my makeup all night and I told everyone you did it. What have you decided about school?" she asked.

DJ surrendered when she looked his way. He had already told her that he would support anything she wanted to do. Though she loved working for the casino, he knew her true love was in doing hair and makeup. He's told her to give her notice several times and leave that job and enroll in school. He could cover their bills while she followed her dream, but he wanted the decision to be hers and not his.

"I'm going to give my notice at the casino and enroll in cosmetology school. I still want to get my college degree. I took an entrance exam to see where I fell and the college admissions advisor told me that I wouldn't have to take any kind of prep classes. She recommended that I submit paperwork to change my GED into a high school diploma. She thinks I can pass that test with no problem. I want to go to college and cosmetology school, but that means I wouldn't be able to work. I don't' want everything to fall on DJ," she said.

"Have I complained?" he asked. "Baby, I want you to do you. I'm doing what I love and I want you to do what you love. I got us covered," he said.

"And if he doesn't, I got you both covered. I want my sister to get and achieve some dreams, too," Jermony said, joining them at the table.

"Sounds to me like you're on your way. The men in your life got you and you know I got you and so does Nichelle and Kimberly if we ever find them. Where is my sister and where is your wife?" Reese asked them.

"Kimberly left to get home to the kids. Our youngest has a cold and she was worried and wanted to get home. I haven't seen your sister," Jermony replied.

"I saw Nichelle. She walked out of the back of the event hall, through the curtains. I thought it was odd, especially when she looked back as if she didn't want anyone to catch her doing so. She slipped out of sight and I came over here," Avalon said.

"Let's go see what she's up to," DJ said to Reese. She's been out of character and we better make sure everything is okay," he added.

"I'm with you," Reese said, standing and joining him.

As they made their way around the outside of the crowd, DJ led the way through the curtains since he knew where the door in the back was located. As they walked down a long narrow hallway, they came upon the sounds of two people giggling behind a door that DJ knew should be locked. He took out his keys which opened every door in the casino and when the door swung open, he almost forgot who the man was who held Nichelle in his arms, kissing her wildly. Pulling them apart, DJ reared his arm back in what he knew was going to be one of the hardest punches he'd ever landed until a strong arm behind him grabbed him before he could put his force behind the punch.

"What the hell!" DJ shouted and turned around where he came face to face with Gary.

"Calm down," Gary told him.

"Really? Your guy has his lips all over my sister and you want me to calm down? You need to tell Councilman Glass to cool off and get the hell away from my sister!" DJ shouted.

Reese stepped up.

"Nichelle? What's going on here and why are you in some closet with Tucker?" she asked.

"Okay, both of you calm down and DJ, don't you dare throw a punch. We are not in the hood anymore!" Nichelle yelled.

"Then, somebody better start explaining or we're all going to the hospital. I know I can't take Gary, but I'm going to rip Tucker here a second one if he doesn't back up from you. He's like, fifteen years older than you!" DJ shouted.

"DJ, stop it and I know how old he is and how old I am. If you calm down long enough, I can explain," Nichelle tried to persuade.

DJ looked to Reese who was nervously tapping her foot and he looked to Tucker who looked like a cat had his tongue. A minute ago, that tongue was all over his sister. He really wanted to knock him out!

"Let me explain," Tucker finally said.

DJ started to jump in when Nichelle raised her hand and stopped them both.

"No, let me," she said to Tucker and then turned around. "I've been seeing Tucker now for about six months. We were going to go public with our relationship after the campaign started and then we found out that we can't go public, but we are still seeing each other. I've been secretly meeting up with him and Gary has been helping us keep it quiet," she explained.

DJ looked around and then his eyes filled with anger landed on Gary.

"Gary? Gary! You've been helping me with Avalon's stuff and you knew about this and didn't say anything? What the hell?" he asked.

"Look, man, this wasn't my story to tell. I'm good at what I do because I keep secrets where I'm supposed to," Gary explained.

"I can't fault that," DJ said, "but I can fault this guy and my sister. Somebody explain all this secrecy," he said.

"My turn," Tucker interjected. "This isn't all on Nichelle to explain. I'm in love with your sister, but I recently found out that I'm officially still married. My divorce was never final, which I didn't know and now my ex-wife won't sign the divorce papers," he explained.

"That's right because it takes two to tangle and the two that will be tangling to the Mayor's mansion is Tucker Glass and me, his wife, Antonia Glass," said a voice behind them all.

All heads turned and all eyes landed on reality television start, Antonia "Roxie" Johnson or Glass depending on who's asking. She was the latest overnight sensation on a locally filmed show called, "One Sister to Another". Everyone knew about the unreal, reality show and the fake drama that's drummed up with each episode. Looks like the drama was about to enter all of their lives.

"Antonia? What are you doing here?" Tucker asked. He wasn't expecting to see her at the event, hoping to put off any further interaction with her until he'd had a chance to figure out the new drama in his life; unexpected drama.

"Okay, this has officially become a circus," Reese joked.

"I'm here because I heard from a reputable source on your staff that you were seeing someone and I'm here to claim my spot as first lady of Chicago. I helped you get here and I intend to reap the benefits or your campaign is dead. Like I said, the two who are tangling will be me and you. Who's ready to toast to that? Tucker, you know where to find me and don't make me wait too long. I don't like to be kept waiting," Antonia shouted and after gulping down the last of the drink she held in her hand, she threw the expensive crystal wine glass to the floor and walked away.

Tucker looked where it broke into a million little pieces and then looked around at everyone, unsure of what to say or do next.

"What in the world is going on?" DJ asked, turning to Reese, hoping she would at least know what to say.

"You're still married to her?" Reese asked Tucker. "I thought that was dead and buried. Have you all seen that show? That chick is crazy. Tuck, you better check around for cameras because that dramatic entrance and exit Ms. Roxie just made was not for our sake. She's up to something and I'm sure it's not pretty," Reese said and laughed.

DJ wasn't finding any of this funny and was pissed that Reese did. Nichelle looked shocked, Tucker looked pissed off and here Reese was laughing like a crazed woman herself.

"If you're married, your hands or any other body part shouldn't be touching my sister, so back up, bro. Seriously, I know you're a councilman and all that, but this is my sister and she doesn't need this kind of drama in her life," DJ said and moved toward Nichelle. When she stepped back from him, he stopped moving.

"Listen, I can't explain it all right now, but I will. Don't ask me to stay away from Nichelle because I can't. I'm in love with her and yes, I may still be married to Antonia, but there has to be a way that I can fix this without dragging Nichelle into anything."

Tucker then turned to Gary.

"What do you need, Councilman?" Gary asked.

"Check to be sure Antonia's show isn't here recording. I don't need that right now," Tucker exclaimed.

"You don't need this right now? You think this is about you and that psycho wife of yours? I've seen the show and fake or real, she likes to keep mess going and they'll be hell to pay if my sister gets hurt," DJ said.

"I can speak for myself!" Nichelle interrupted. "Stop speaking as if I'm not here. Tucker explained everything to me and I'm okay with it. He'll get a divorce and everything will be fine," Nichelle said, leaning over to take Tucker's hand, holding it tight.

This time DJ did laugh, but not as loud as Reese had done.

"Nichelle, that shows your immaturity. Did you not see Antonia just fly through here? I think she's made it clear that nothing is about to be easy and you're going to get caught in the middle. Are you ready for your business to be out in the public, getting scrutinized and made fun of? That's what will happen and if I'm correct, Antonia will spin everything in her favor. Back away, sis. I'm telling you to back away," DJ pleaded. "Reese, help me here. Tell her this isn't going to end well," he added.

"I don't know what's going on or what will happen, but I have been where Nichelle is, wanting a man that may not be hers, but look at her – she's not backing away from Tucker and right now isn't the time to deal with this. There are a lot of people here tonight and we need to get back out there. This Antonia chick? I remember her and she's always been about a bunch of mess and I'm sure we haven't seen the last of her. I have to say, I already like her spunk, though. She came in here and stole the entire scene. I guess being on a reality show has taught her a lot about garnering her audience," Reese said.

"Look, I'll take care of this. Thanks, Reese, for being on our side," Tucker said.

Reese sucked her teeth and turned to him.

"Oh, do not mistake what is going on here. I love my sister and she has no business with you. Stay away from her, Tucker, until you are no longer a married man and from the looks of things, this tangle just got interesting!" Reese exclaimed and walked in the same direction as Antonia had.

DJ was left standing with his mouth wide open trying to find the right words.

"That's it, Reese? That's all you're going to say and where are you going? We need to talk some sense into Nichelle," he said and hoped that Reese' pause before finally leaving meant that he would have her to depend on with this. He still wanted to hurt Tucker, but he didn't want to make a bigger scene than Antonia had.

"I have learned to let adults live their lives their way and Tucker knows me. He's known me a long time. I'm surprised he's hooked up with our sister, but Nichelle knows to reach out if she needs us. Right now, I want to see if there are cameras recording her show. I secretly watch every episode, but not one of them is as wild and crazy as the mess that goes on with the brothers in this town. It's non-stop craziness. I just love all the drama in Chicago! You brothers in Chi-Town are *fire!*" she added before disappearing behind the black curtain.

DJ wasn't intrigued. He didn't want his sister tangled up with some married man and his outlandish wife. He'd just gotten out of dealing with his own brand of drama and knew he didn't want the same for his sister. He started to say something when Tucker pulled Nichelle to the side and they began to whisper. She may not understand it, but the web she was now tangled up in with Tucker and Antonia was only the beginning.

Coming up next – book 5 in "The Brothers of Chi-Town" series, "It Takes Two to Tangle"

Councilman Tucker Glass, a native of Chicago, has set his eyes on the biggest prize, that of Mayor of the city he has loved all of his life. At thirty-nine, his career spans back many years as a City Council member and then most recently, as City Council President. His resume reads like a ratings-topper novel full of accomplishments that make him more than qualified for the job, but what he wants to avoid is the drama that could block his path to the Mayor's mansion. He's always been a strait-laced politician, but his personal life could spawn a real-life reality show complete with hair pulling, tongue-lashing and accusatory finger pointing which would all occur in the first episode.

Tucker wasn't expecting his past to come back to haunt him just as he'd found the woman who was making his life complete. He would do anything to keep her in his life, but is he willing to give up his run for the Mayor's office to keep that love in-tact?

Nichelle Michaels didn't know that love could be so right until she met and fell in love with Tucker Glass, a man fourteen years older and wiser than her, but who showed her how a man should treat a woman, and that's after she spent the past year testing the water between how a man loves and how a woman loves. Now that she knows what she wants, a woman from Tucker's past could ruin her perfect love.

Tucker and Nichelle are in love, but is he willing to risk his chance at being Mayor because his ex-wife, or the woman he thought was his ex-wife, wants to now be First Lady of Chicago? Was he really ready to tangle with a woman who specialized in drama every day on television as the star on the nation's number one reality show?

Tucker may be ready for Chicago, but is Chicago ready for the drama that comes along with the popular politician?

Find out in, *"It Takes Two to Tangle"*, book 5 in the series. Preorder available now at www.cherylbarton.net

Upcoming Release

Girl Dad,

A Dramatic and Inspirational Novel by Cheryl Barton

Cyrus Jackson spent a life focused on his own wants, needs and desires and he didn't care who he had to hurt to get what he wanted. He is a Washington, D.C. local gangster, hoodlum and at one time, drug king-pin, known to put gut-wrenching fear into the hearts and minds of everyone he encountered, never letting his feelings get in the way of being on top of his game. He has a family he was estranged from, choosing instead to create a new family from friends who were loyal to the death to him. He'd been in and out of jail since his teenage years and spent his adult years surviving by any means necessary. He is feared by many, hated by even more and was known to have a heart that was ice-cold and unfeeling. He was the last person anyone expected to turn into a #GirlDad after finding out about an orphaned daughter he never knew he had.

Little Shiloh Moore entered Cyrus' life and with one look, his heart swelled with a love he never knew he could possess. He saw a little girl who needed someone to save her and most of all, love her. Cyrus wanted a fresh start, a chance to prove he could be the father that Shiloh needed in her life even when a system that knows of his past is hesitant to let him prove that he could change.

Cyrus and Shiloh had an uphill battle of trust and love ahead of them, but Cyrus was determined to be the best dad he never knew how to be, but was willing to learn because Shiloh was worth every sacrifice of him getting away from who he thought he needed to be in order to make it in the world, to become a man who wanted nothing more than to put her first. He didn't have to convince himself, but with a past like his, it was everyone else who needed convincing that he was no longer the self-serving bastard he was always known to be.

In no time at all, Cyrus saw himself becoming a #GirlDad and he's never wanted anything more than to be just that to a little girl who stole his heart with just one look.

Cyrus was set to make major changes in his life to make room for his daughter, but his past wasn't ready to let him go. The fierce protector in him was willing to give up any and everything for the little girl who turned him into a #GirlDad.

Preorder your copy now at www.cherylbarton.net

Make sure you check out book 1, of "The Brothers of Chi-Town", *I Can't Let Go* – now available for download and in paperback.
https://www.amazon.com/dp/B07FK477CN

www.cherylbarton.net

Carter Garrison vowed to love, honor and cherish his wife, Sienna, forsaking all others, something he forgot to do during a weekend of fun, bad company and poor judgement.

Sienna Garrison never dreamed her college sweetheart, Carter, whom she pledged her life to, would break her heart and when he did, she moved out and moved on - or tried to.

What better occasion is there than a friend's wedding to stir up old feelings and memories of love, intense passion and nights of sensual titillation. Gazes from across a room after almost two years apart revealed depths of love that had never died.

Seeing Sienna again reminded Carter of what he'd lost and he vowed to never let go by doing whatever he could to get his wife back even if it included begging and pleading. Is Sienna ready to forgive and take a chance on life again with the only man she'd ever really loved?

When Carter brings on the charm and turns up the heat, no woman is immune, especially Sienna.

Don't forget to snag your copy of book 2, *Swagger and Baggage*, in "The Brothers of Chi-Town" series – now available at https://www.amazon.com/dp/B07VKN6M12

www.cherylbarton.net

It's not a coincidence that casino owner, Torrence Allen, ran into his college sweetheart, Reese Michaels again; it's fate. As his memories unfold, he had tried everything to keep her in his life and his bed back then and failed at both. She wasn't ready for him then, but he hopes she is ready for him now.

Reese Michaels never thought she'd see Torrence again. Their split in college was dramatic and hurtful and still, no man had been able to win her heart. She considered herself the permanent third wheel to friends who had found love and marriage.

Their whirlwind affair, quickly turned into love just as it suddenly crashed and burned when a woman shows up to claim Torrence as hers. When it's also revealed that this woman isn't the only 'other woman', Reese finds herself left with a broken heart, shattered love and dreams of forever beyond her reach. How did she not know about the other part of Torrence's active and amorous life?

Torrence isn't ready to give up on having Reese in his life after his deceit. He finds himself in the fight of his life to finally have the love and commitment he wanted only with her. His swagger had always won women over, but it's his baggage that's causing his life to spiral out of control and he could once again find himself without the woman he has always loved.

Pick up, book 3, of "The Brothers of Chi-Town" series, *Claiming His Child* – now available for download and in paperback.

https://www.amazon.com/Claiming-Child-Brothers-Chi-Town-Book-ebook/dp/B07YJVMN49/ref=sr_1_1?keywords=claiming+barton&qid=1583955090&sr=8-1

www.cherylbarton.net

Business magnate Dexter Patterson refused to let anything keep him from checking off all of the boxes equating to achievement in life to prove that though he came from a rough childhood on the south side of Chicago, he still thrived and became a success. Looking around at those closest to him, Dexter found that he was still missing something...Love.

When aspiring model, Alyssa Kincaid met Dexter, she couldn't get enough of his sexual magnetism, fiery nights of passion, and secret rendezvous. She thought they were headed toward forever when a surprising call from him ended what they had causing her to leave Chicago, taking with her a secret.

Dexter thought that no woman could ever tame him, not even Alyssa who entranced him with her sexy body, smoky, sultry voice and untamed desire. Too little, too late, he realized he'd made a mistake by walking away and then she was gone.

Time and distance didn't diminish the chemistry between them and the child Alyssa carried and never told him about had him in the fight of his life to win back her heart and the chance to have the family he'd always wanted.

Will Alyssa continue to curse kismet when Dexter suddenly reappears in her life or will she believe that his yearning for her isn't just because of their child, but because when she left Chicago, she took his heart with her?

Now available – New Release
Book 3, "Heartbreaker" of "A Lovers" Heart Series
https://www.amazon.com/dp/B07WH7Z2KR

www.cherylbarton.net

In book 3, of "A Lovers' Heart" steamy romance series, Cameron Lymon, the sexy, youngest brother of Hollywood heartthrob, Cade Weston and Navy SEAL, Calvin Lymon, with his Master's degree in Journalism and a minor in Communications and Sports Management in hand, landed his dream job in Denver, Colorado as the co-host for a new morning talk show. Women love to call him the "Heartbreaker" because of the bevy of beautiful ladies he's left in his wake, not interested in giving up being a bachelor for falling in love. He enjoys taking after his big brother's old lifestyle of being a playboy.

Dakota Kane sacrificed a personal life and fought hard in her career to be the lead personality on Denver's top television morning show, but she was about to risk it all for passionate, steamy encounters with her new, much younger co-host, who is ten years younger and fifty shades hotter than any man she'd ever encountered. All he had to do was smile at her and she was a goner.

Cameron didn't know what he was in for when what he thought would be casual, behind closed door romps with the ever-so-sexy Dakota began to turn into much more when his heart became as invested in her as much as his body had. As things turned serious, his heartbreaker status came back to haunt him and his relationship with Dakota was threatened by his past.

Cameron and Dakota have to decide if what they are beginning to feel for each other is worth the risk of their careers when their secret love affair becomes the topic of public opinion and ridicule.

The Lake House

Summers together at their families' lake houses as teenagers are what Danielle Fenton and the boy next door, Gannon Wilcox, loved about being on the lake in North Carolina. They fell in love at a young age and then one day it was over after Danielle ended their relationship with no explanation. The only thing Gannon remembered was seeing the woman he loved in the arms of another man.

Years later, Danielle and Gannon find themselves back at the lake, in their families' lake houses, both divorced after unhappy marriages and trying to find their next moves. They now have a chance to get this thing called love right as long as they believe in the history and power of love found at the lake that was always meant to be everlasting.

My First Love

Ethan Bennett has what everyone wished they had, money, power and respect. When his first love, Valencia, walks back into his life, the love they shared as teenagers resurfaces and reminds him that there is no love like that first love.

Valencia Ramos never forgot the first person who loved her unconditionally. Now all grown up, Ethan is still everything she ever wanted and the love she still feels for him is a love she's never been able to forget.

Discover their path to finding out if first love is truly real love.

Leo Westmoreland is an ordinary guy living in Harlem, New York, working three jobs to make ends meet the best way he can in order to take care of his mother and younger brothers years after his abusive father disappeared from their lives. He hasn't been lucky in love, finding most women want more when it comes to material things than he has available to give. He has dreams and aspirations for himself, but for now, family comes first.

Raquel Johnson was born with a silver spoon in her mouth to a father who owns one of the top money management firms in Manhattan. Though she's never wanted for anything, she's made her own achievements in life and now sits as an executive with his company. Her dating life has consisted of men who value money, power and prestige over unconditional love, the one thing she desires the most.

Leo and Raquel meet and share a connection that breathes new life into them and proves that focusing on each other and the love they can have together is more important than anything else.

Read Leo and Raquel's story and discover that love and relationships are about who you are, not what you have.

And Then There Was You
https://www.amazon.com/dp/B07GJG1HVN

www.cherylbarton.net

"And Then There Was You," is a steamy love story, set in Malibu, California. Diezel Wilder is a sexy corporate attorney from New York who recently moved to California after a bitter divorce from a woman he married on a whim after going through a tragedy that caused him to act out. In need of a break from the drama that surrounded him in New York, he hoped for a new start in sunny California.

Brooklyn Hunter, a sexy Armenian bombshell, is a late-night, on-air radio talk show host who woos men all over the country with her sexy, sultry, seductive voice. She's coming off of a divorce from a movie studio executive who is twenty years older. When they met, she saw him as her escape from a dismal life in Nebraska, but found herself thrust into the Hollywood spotlight, revealing a marriage clouded by adultery and out of wedlock children in a scandal that was broadcast worldwide.

Seeking a new lease on life, Diezel and Brooklyn are in search of the kind of connection with a mate that leaves them breathless. Little did they know they would find it right next door.

Bring on the ice-cold water because you're about to go on one very steamy ride to love in, "And Then There Was You."

The Bachelor Series
www.cherylbarton.net

Book 1 - Bachelor Not for Sale – Now available

Duron Knight agreed to take part in a bachelor auction held by his sister's sorority. Little did he know that he would find the woman of his dreams in the form of sexy bombshell Taija Charles, the woman in red.

Taija, in a room full of the sexiest men in Atlanta, has eyes for one handsome bachelor that no woman in her right mind could resist.

As sparks fly between them, can Duron put his unhappy past with women behind him and give his all to Taija? He may fight love, but Taija has plans to help him mend his broken heart with real love and a whole lot of lust.

About the Author

Cheryl Barton lives in Maryland and in her spare time she loves to read espionage, crime and romance novels, cook, watch Sci-fi movies, spend time with family and friends and enjoy Maryland steamed crabs. Cheryl is celebrating 30 years as a government employee and loves writing romance novels when she's not working. Cheryl is the author of 31 romance novels, 3 inspirational novels and is proud of 4 book compilation projects with several other incredible women called, "One Sister Away: Encouraging Words from One Sister to Another" – a series of books meant to encourage, empower and inspire other women. People often ask Cheryl which book is her favorite of all of those she's written. While she finds it hard to select one favorite, Cheryl still looks to her first novel, Bachelor Not for Sale, if she had to pick a favorite because it was her first novel and the one that inspired her to continue writing.

Cheryl was a 2019 Finalist for the Emma Award given by Romance Slam Jam and a 2018 Finalist for the Literary Trailblazer of the Year award by the Indie Author Legacy Award. Cheryl is a member of the Romance Writers of America – National Chapter, the Maryland Romance Writers and the Contemporary Romance Writers groups, the Black Writers' Guild of Maryland and the International Women Writers Guild.

Indulge in more romance and inspirational novels by visiting her website at www.cherylbarton.net and connect with Cheryl on Facebook, Twitter and Instagram @cherylbartonbooks